STORIES OF MAGIC AND ENCHANTMENT

BY

WILLIAM R MISTELE

Falcon Books Publishing

TITLES BY WILLIAM MISTELE

williammistele.com

Undines: Lessons from the Realm of the Water Spirits (North Atlantic Books, 2011)
Mermaids, Sylphs, Gnomes, and Salamanders (North Atlantic Books, 2012)

Forthcoming Titles

El—The Biography of a Pleiadian
Mermaid Tales
Problems in the Study of Mermaids
Ten Rules for Spiritual Beginners
The Perfection of Wisdom—A Guide to Establishing Justice on Earth

To view other works:

Video poems - Williammistele.com/videopoems.html
Website: Williamrmistele.com
Contact: pyrhums@yahoo.com

Stories of Magic and Enchantment

By

William R. Mistele

Falcon Books Publishing
(2017)

Cover art by Rostik Balash Printed in the United States of America.

2017 First Edition Published by
Falcon Books Publishing

www.falconbookspublishing.com
First Printing: 2017

ISBN-13: 978-9869492508

To have another by your side who is with you, who feels what you feel, and who dreams your dreams—is this not the greatest mystery of life?

DEDICATION

I would like to dedicate this book to those who celebrate the awe, wonder, and beauty of life. Though horror, suffering, and darkness are ever present, love appears offering endless opportunities to transform ourselves and the world.

ACKNOWLEDGMENTS

I would like to thank the Czech magician, Franz Bardon, who put his own life at risk many times in order to reveal a host of magical teachings to our world. Much of what I write is a direct result of practicing his meditations. For example, my section on Creation Stories is inspired by his teachings on the creative power of the spoken word and Kabbalah.

I would like to thank my mother and my father. Between them they embodied many of the core conflicts and also the great opportunities the twentieth century offered to those who have sought to better themselves and others.

My deepest appreciation goes to Tanya Robinson for her great enthusiasm and clarity of mind in guiding this book into publication.

And, though it may sound odd to our ears, much of my inspiration derives from direct contact with spirits of the Earthzone and the spirits within the realms hidden within nature belonging to Salamanders, Mermaids, Sylphs, and Gnomes. Occasionally, one of these spirits will drop by as I mediate and suggested I write something that celebrates its perspective on life.

PREFACE

These stories range from the distant past to the far future, from the time of Neanderthal to later on when Homo sapiens have long departed. They take place in mythical kingdoms like Atlantis and Ubarim. There are discussions between angels and meetings with celestial administrators. There are trees that speak and magical beings like trolls, gnomes, elves, sylphs, and mermaids.

The Creator himself has to defend his creation and negotiate with humans to produce mutually satisfying solutions. Some stories take place in dreams. In some the dead speak and the departed have a few last words before they go into the light. Some stories occur in alternate realities or on distant worlds. In one, a robot discusses his sentience.

We encounter enlightened beings. We wrestle with angels. And we watch as Magi try to cope with the appearance of a new religion. We tour an ancient Temple of Saturn. And we listen to stories of an ancient order of women whose magic brings masculine and feminine into balance.

There is a reason for the diversity of locations in time and space. For me human beings do not yet know what they are. Human nature as of yet has no clear definition. Our options as a species are wide open.

My stories strongly suggest we are surrounded by infinite possibilities. We face great dangers. We are often on the edge of extinction. And yet it is quite possible we will not only survive but soon have colonies in nearby solar systems.

Yet underneath the dazzling array of choices we have yet to make lies one theme—the joining of love and power. What would it be if we felt one with our lovers, that is, if we discover how to overcome all barriers that separate one from another? What would it be if we held others and the world itself within our hearts, caring for nature and for all living beings as much as we care for our own children?

All these stories are as real for me as if I had lived through them in lucid dreams. Most appear in my mind as I meditate. Like the prisoner in the first story, at night when I dream I often dream not my own but other people's dreams.

Do gnomes, mermaids, sylphs, and salamanders have any reality? You can read some of my other books about such beings and draw your own conclusions. In this book, I have tried to entertain. And yet when I meditate, I can feel a part of any being and dream its innermost dreams. Accompany me on a journey in which we search for the deepest treasures within the heart.

TABLE OF CONTENTS

INTRODUCTION

The stories in this book are divided into six parts: Dreams, the Mythical Land of Atlantis, Creation, Science Fiction, Children's Stories, and Celestial Bureaucracy.

Magic operates on principles that science has not yet discovered. Enchantment is pleasure refined to the level of bliss, ecstasy, and rapture. And from such refined pleasures arise dreams and visions.

I do in depth interviews with individuals who repeatedly experience things that science cannot explain. For example, they not only lucid dream in which they are aware that they are dreaming; different individuals recall sharing the same dream with each other. While dreaming, they also visit and observe what is going on in other places in our world.

For many of these individuals, their dream lives are more real to them than their lives here in this world. And yet they have learned that the inner world and the outer world are not separate. A dream well dreamed becomes reality. In the not distant future, this kind of enchantment will be taught in universities.

Part I: Dreams

In the story, The Prisoner, an individual is in jail, but because his dreams have attained a high level of perception, he sees into the deepest secrets of other's souls. When he sleeps at night, he dreams not his own but other people's dreams as well. Watch how he converts the art of dreaming into a way of getting out of jail.

In A Knight and a Mermaid, a knight wakes up in another kind of reality and struggles to comprehend its nature. Love is thick in the air. There is no violence since peace is everywhere. And separation does not exist, for to be conscious is to be equally conscious of other's thoughts and feelings with the same clarity with which you are aware of your own.

In the story Farmer Jack Allen and the Sylph, a sylph, an air spirit who dwells in the sky, takes on flesh and blood. Now what is it about this farmer that has enchanted her to come down and spend a year with a mortal who lives on a farm?

In A Sailor and his Lover, a man and a woman discover they can create an entire world where they live together within their shared dream. But at what point does this shared dream become so real that it becomes reality?

In The Carrier Strike Group Commander and the Mermaid, a man and a mermaid fall in love. But what kind of dream must you create so that individuals from separate evolutions can become one with each other? Imagine—to command more fire power than has existed in all the wars fought on earth. Yet to love a woman from another realm may require a different kind of command over oneself.

In ancient Rome, when you entered any temple, you entered that temple's dreams. In the story, The Temple of Saturn, we encounter nightmares, sorrow, and loss. And yet in the heart of this temple is a dream in which we attain absolute freedom.

In the story, James O'Brien, a man who has died discovers that he still dreams. But now his dreams enable him to walk among the living and perceive what makes them feel alive. And he observes that some of the living to some extent are already dead. Being perceptive enables James O'Brien to live in two different worlds at the same time.

In the story, The Oracle, a mafia don learns that he does not have to wait until he is dead to experience a "life review." The Oracle, with perfect detachment and acceptance, walks the mafia don through the life he has lived up to this point in time. And, as the Oracle asks him questions, the don discovers for himself what has been missing from his life—for now he meets the part of himself he has never known—the person he was always meant to be.

In the story, A Magical Attack: A Retelling, a Tibetan lama knows a secret. Whether you are alive or dead, there is no need to define your identity through attachment to any form. For this lama, consciousness is without form or image. And, knowing this, nothing negative or malicious can exert any influence over him.

In the story, Lugnas the Peacemaker, Lugnas embodies a dream of peace. His dream is so powerful that hostility and aggression dissolve in his presence. Now people have every right to be negative. After all, a basic spiritual principle is that you cannot interfere with another's free will. But the people in the world of Lugnas learn another spiritual principle—it is impossible to be negative when Lugnas is in town.

Part II: Dreams Continued

Here are stories of Buddha walking down the road and meeting various individuals. Buddha is not just enlightened. His empathy is so great that he perceives others as himself in another form. Now what happens to great warriors, scoundrels, mermaids, and wounded lovers when they meet someone like that?

In The Time Machine, a man takes a ride into the future to discover the kind of woman he really needs.

In the story, On Becoming a Man, a son asks his father for the wisdom he will need in order to grow up and become a man. Sometimes a dream is passed from one generation to another. But if that dream fails to blossom, it is then left to next generation to find a new beginning.

In the story, The Astral Plane, a man is disturbed by his obsession with women. He considers his situation hopeless. But the astral plane takes on the form of a woman and has a conversation with him. Let's see how he overcomes his obsession with attractive women to discover the true nature of love.

Part III: Atlantis

In the section on Atlantis, there are stories about an ancient Order of women. This secret Order discovers how to overcome darkness in the world. They do so by entering the dreams of the most powerful men on earth. For five thousand years, they succeed in changing malice into nobility and hatred into love. Surely, it is left to our world to carry on their work.

Here too in Atlantis we meet two different women who have learned a sacred dance. Within this dance they are able to embody the deepest dreams of the planet earth.

Part IV: Creation

Want to upgrade your dreams in life, whether lucid or otherwise? Take a look at the section called Creation Stories.

In the story, The Prime Directive, an angel argues with the Creator that he is already a perfect being. But no. More is required him. He has to become a human being in order to discover for himself the ultimate purpose of creation.

In A Council of Angels, angels try to resolve a problem in working with human beings. What are the mysterious purposes underlying the creation of the earth, the sky, and the seas? Listen in and discover what is hidden in the Creator's deepest dreams.

In the story, Shekinah, a woman discusses with the Creator why the Creator's plans keep failing. Yet because she persists in demanding a solution that works, she receives from the Creator more than anyone has ever received before.

Entering recorded history, we have the story, Balaam, the Gentile Prophet. Balaam is hired by King Balak of the Moabites to counter the threat of an Israeli invasion. According to the Bible, Balaam had the power to curse and to bless nations. For Balaam, changing history was as easy as a prince at court whispering the right words at the right time into the right ears. This magic is still available, though in this age of the world anyone using it must be far more circumspect.

Dreams do not just belong to individuals. Different races such as Neanderthal and Homo sapiens, through their actions and their dreams, create original destinies for themselves. Each race gets to choose what part it wishes play in the unfolding of the universe. Where does that leave Homo sapiens?

Part V: Science Fiction

In the section on Science Fiction, we observe individuals who are masters of their own and of other's dreams as well. Skill on this level can change the history of the world. In the story of The Queen, a woman decides to change the history of the entire galaxy.

Part VI: Children's Stories

In the section of Children's Stories, we enter the dreams of trees, elves, gnomes, dragons, and trolls. Everything has a dream inside if you pause and listen, if you take the time to perceive without thoughts intervening.

Consider the story of St. Patrick and the Elves. In this story, the dreams of the human realm and of the Blessed Realm collide. It might take more than a saint to reconcile the differences.

Part VII: Celestial Bureaucracy

In the section, we meet individuals who seek divine assistance in enriching their dreams. In the story, The Akashic Department of Fairy Kingdoms, a man decides he wants to upgrade his dream world so it becomes an authentic fairy kingdom.

Now if you were to do this, would you want to populate your magical realm with creatures of your own imagination? Or will you want to invite others such as your friends to become members of your fairy kingdom?

Note: In the future, some of these stories may become parts of novels I plan to write. I have added them to this book since they wanted to be read sooner rather than later.

PART I

DREAMS I

Aprisoner in a penitentiary is assigned yard duty. As he goes through the door leading to the yard he happens to pass the warden walking in the opposite direction. And he stops and says to the warden, "I am glad you had a good time at your son David's birthday party yesterday.

"The warden glances harshly into the eyes of the prisoner and asks, "How did you know about his birthday party?"

The prisoner replies, "Like Joseph in the dungeon of the Pharaoh of Egypt, God has given me the ability to see the past, present, and future in my dreams. And last night that is what I dreamed."

The warden takes the prisoner to his private office. He has him sit down in the chair facing his desk. And then the warden asks, "Answer me this. Why am I so unhappy?"

The prisoner replies, "Your oldest brother is a U.S. senator and your middle brother runs his own successful hedge fund. He has a second home in Aspen and a third home in Italy. And he attends the Cannes Film Festival where the independent films he sponsors sometimes win high honors.

"But neither of your brothers is genuinely happy. To be happy is to feel free in your soul."

The warden asks rhetorically, "Is a convict in my prison about to explain to me what it is to be free?"

The prisoner answers "To make the most out of life is like looking in a mirror and the person you see is your favorite character in a movie, someone you have always wanted to be. Your presence makes others feel more alive."

The warden summarizes, "Detached like you are on the outside looking in and yet treating each moment as if something new and wonderful is happening.

"Exactly," says the prisoner.

The warden sends the man back to his yard duty, though from time to time they have a quiet conversation. Six months later the prisoner is pardoned by the governor. A limousine waits for him outside the gate the day he is released. He is taken to meet the governor.

As it turned out, the night after talking to the warden the prisoner dreamed about a personal problem of the governor's. He told the warden about this dream. The warden passed that information on to the governor explaining what the prisoner had already told him about what it is to feel free.

Later, the man's story reaches the ears of a publisher who is so impressed he advances a substantial sum for the man to write a book about how he was released from prison. Sitting in the publisher's office, his editor asks him, "What is the secret of your luck?"

And man replies, "When you are so receptive there is nothing inside yourself to interfere with what you are seeing, then you feel a part of everyone. Usually when people dream at night their dreams are about their own lives. But when I sleep, I dream other people's dreams. And when I do this I see how things can turn out better for them with a few minor changes."

The editor says, "When you dream tonight, dream of me."

The year is 1307. The Church, in great treachery and malice, seeks to destroy all of the Knights Templar throughout Europe. A few manage to escape.

The knight gazes upon his own body lying next to a small stream in a green field at the edge of a mountain cliff. He turns and looks at a young woman sitting next to him.

He says to her, "I am dead and you are an angel."

She replies, "You are not dead and I am not an angel."

He looks about himself at the hills, the trees, the stream, the forest, the sky and clouds. He says, "Each thing here shines with its own inner light. The colors here are a thousand times brighter and clearer than they are in my world."

"I have heard others say the se same words," she replies.

The knight responds, "And you—the light within you flows through me even as this stream. This is a very unusual dream."

"It is not a dream," she says calmly.

The knight goes on, "It is like you and the stream are the same energy, the same being. And you and I are also the same energy, the same being.

"Tell me, child of the mysteries, in what world, in what reality does beauty such as this exist? Tell me so that when I awaken in my body I may make it my life quest to find this place again, to find you again that we might be even as we are now."

"You are a human being," she replies. "I am from a race that by God's grace does not require spoken words to express feelings, does not need medicine in order to heal, and we do not require passion or compassion in order to love.?

"But you must speak words to express yourself and what you feel. Speak aloud now what you sense this place to be. Speak, so that when you return to yourself you will know this is not a dream and you will remember everything you have heard and seen."

The knight says,

The stream begins
Where the clouds drift
Enfolding the hills in mist
Moisture so thick
The waters run wild
Dancing in the rain like a child
The current, the pulse, the flow,
Here are secrets only love knows—
How to be one with another's soul.

Knight: "Will you speak to me again? Will you come to me and guide me? Will you be to me even as you are now, part of my own being?"

She replies, "As the sky is a part of the stream, and the earth, and the valley; as the stream nurtures all things, even so I shall be a part of your soul. Forever free, in love and in beauty, as one stream our lives shall unfold."

The farmer's name was Jack Allen. He had a story to tell, but some stories you cannot share with friends, or even family.

Farmer Jack Allen owned a farm of four hundred and ninety acres. Oh, there were enough trees in the Northwest corner to call it a woods. And there was a stream with an old covered bridge. The bridge was nice for pictures, but not sturdy enough to drive a tractor across.

Jack Allen's farm had a barn. The silo was big enough. And decades before he had a horse.

He had a few chickens and two hogs. Done with cows. Had enough of milking cows when he was young.

He mostly grew corn and barley. Hired some help in the fall during harvest. No mortgage or liens. Father and grandfather had been frugal and diligent. His siblings lived on the coasts, east and west. Off to seek fortune or live in friendly cities where you can stroll around down town.

He had a wife once, but she ran off. A woman does not make a good farmer's wife if she is troubled by silence or the absence of entertaining company.

Not much more to say about farmer Jack Allen other than he enjoyed his life. His favorite activity was sitting out on the porch watching the sunset. There he sometimes saw his cat hunting, which is done best during twilight. And he would wait for the moon to rise, if it did so before 9 o'clock.

Now no one else would know to tell you—because it is not something you can observe. But, as he sat there during twilight for an hour or so each night, not a single thought passed through his mind.

Oh he was aware of the breeze in the trees, leaves shaking, the roof occasionally creaking, the thump of the cat at it leaped, the caw of a crow, and the crops whispering as they moved to and fro.

But these sounds found no mental response on his part. He just did not feel a need to interpret, comment, or respond to what he perceived.

Now living as he did in tornado alley the barometer can fall. The sky goes dark. Temperature drops. The wind picks up and begins to howl. Sometimes large hail stones rain down. Not good for the crops.

It happened almost too fast to grasp. A huge black cloud hovered over his house. He saw torn trees tossing about a quarter mile away. And amid a huge curtain of flailing rain, a tornado was touching down. But where he sat on his porch the wind barely stirred though there was the beginning of a very strong updraft.

Too sudden to run to the storm shelter, Jack Allen headed toward the basement. But before he had has hand on the door knob, the tornado was gone.

The sky cleared. The light grew bright in the windows. And then he heard a sound from the front porch like a child crying. He stepped through the front door. To his left, a girl was curled up on a couch on his porch. She was a young women, maybe nineteen, without a stitch of clothing on her.

He brought her in. She seemed quite disoriented. Couldn't talk. Moaning softly. Eyes dilated. And her body temperature was cold as if she had been walking through snow.

He set her down on the couch. Drew a blanket tight around her. Found her some clothes. Heated up some coffee and held her close to warm her up. All very gentlemanly.

She soon fell asleep. He didn't know what to do. Phones were out. Roads no doubt were blocked.

In the morning to his surprise she seemed content and happy. Except she did not know how to talk or write and so she had no name to give him. He went to make breakfast and she followed him and stood and watched as he scrambled eggs, toasted some muffins, and spread them with butter and blackberry jam.

They sat at the table together and, by gum, farmer Jack Allen had to teach her how to use a knife and fork. He really did not know what to make of her except she seemed extraordinarily happy. And for farmer Jack Allen seeing happiness in a woman was a very rare occasion.

Now you might wonder about what happens next. Put simply Jack kept the girl. Why would he do that? After all, Jack Allen is a normal, down to earth, and honest kind of guy.

Perhaps in the back of his mind he thought to himself, "Damn. Maybe once or twice in a life as stark raving ordinary as mine there comes a genuine surprise. And I am not about to share it, not if it's a woman who is as happy as this woman and who seems to have no desire to be anywhere else than here with me."

Or maybe Jack knew what few on earth know—that life's greatest secret is that she is full of surprises. And when these surprises come you do not want to waste them. In any case, some things you just don't tell other people, not your friends, or even your family.

She stayed a year. And over those twelve months she learned to talk. But Jack Allen rarely needed to say anything to her. If Jack Allen had known the word telepathy he would have said, "She reads my mind as easily as a sailor can read a red sky at dawn or a barometer registers air pressure. She knows what is going on."

They were never intimate, though it was not like she was a daughter or a sister. I say that because she would cuddle up to him as they sat out on the porch during twilight. And when she did that he felt as if gravity had switched off. He felt he was floating, weightless. He was sitting on the porch but he might as well have been twenty thousand feet up in the sky looking down at the world below. It was the kind of relaxation few men on earth will ever feel, even if they sky dive or are astronauts in a space station. There was simply nothing weighing upon him.

There is not much more to tell you. What I describe is how it went every day. He worked as usual. She cooked, cleaned, and did a few chores. And every single thing she did he had to teach her from scratch. She simply did not have a clue. But like I said she learned very quickly and that you can do if reading minds is natural to you.

Farmer Jack Allen had a premonition. He dreamed one night she took off her clothes and walked out the front door and in this world she was no more.

And that is what happened a few days later. Another dark cloud appeared from nowhere. A great funnel descended. Again, the eye of a huge tornado surrounded the farm house and barn. And she walked through the door and was gone.

The cloud vanished. The sun came out. The sky quickly cleared.

And for years after that winter always came late and spring early. The rain was always right, never too much to flood the stream, actually just enough to produce the best harvest.

Farmer Jack Allen still sits on his porch at twilight. And sometimes he feels the girl is right there sitting beside him, cuddling up to him. He did not think any of this was strange, weird, or bizarre. As I mentioned before, farmer Jack Allen had a most peculiar mental ability—he didn't think at all when he sat at twilight watching the sun set or the moon rise later on.

And the kicker was that when he felt she was there with him he would get that weightless sensation of being so relaxed there was nothing on earth that could bother him.

It has been a few years since farmer Jack Allen found a naked teenage girl on his porch. He kept her for a year and then she mysteriously disappeared. Well, won't you know? It happened again.

During the night there was a thunderstorm and lightning striking a few hundred yards out. But when that storm hit, Jack Allen was not concerned. He rolled over in bed and went back to sleep.

So then morning comes. The storm is gone and the dark indigo of night is just beginning to fade. Odd thing is that if Jack Allen didn't know better he could have sworn that the birds had been up early singing at least two hours before dawn. There was a goldfinch chirping and a group of doves cooing. Most odd.

Jack Allen steps through the front door and finds a girl curled up on the couch he has on his porch. She is wearing tight fitting blue jeans torn with a blood trail going down one leg beneath the knee. And a nose bleed has left a dark stain on her magenta T-shirt.

She is nineteen or twenty. Blue eyes, dark hair cut short; maybe she is ninety pounds and say five foot four. But this time no storm cell accompanies the girl's sudden appearance.

Jack Allen bends down and asks the girl, "You okay?"

The girl waves her hand as if to say, "Go away." She closes her eyes and goes back to sleep.

Jack Allen gets a wash cloth, some antiseptic, a few large band-aids, and tape. He rolls up her left leg blue jean and washes her abrasions. She doesn't complain. Just lies there. He cuts the sticky ends off the band-aids and tapes them onto her leg. No need for stitches. He fetches a blanket and covers her with it.

Two hours later the girl comes limping through the front door into the house and sits down at the table, head in her hands. Jack

Allen, figuring she is hungry, makes some scrambled eggs and toast and sets it before her. She helps herself.

Now just to be clear so there is no confusion, Jack Allen is now retired and, like before, he enjoys living alone. You could say he is a low maintenance kind of guy. Now, as you already know, the highlight of his day is still sitting on the porch watching the sun rise and later in the day watching it set again. And when he sits there watching, not a single thought goes through his mind. Perhaps in that one way only—in regard to his mental processes—farmer Jack Allen is a most unusual man.

All the same, as we already know, Jack Allen understands that life is full of surprises. And maybe when you know this secret about life, life throws a few extra surprises your way. All of which is to say, though Jack Allen is a true gentleman, he does enjoy on rare occasions such as this the company of a young woman.

After she is done eating, he says to the girl, "My name is Jack Allen. You are ....?"

It takes two more days before she tells him her name—Theresa. She doesn't say much more than that. But she is helpful. On the second day, she takes out the garbage, cooks breakfast and dinner. Funny though, some days she only eats a carrot and a strawberry or two.

She also washes the dishes. Does the laundry. Sweeps the leaves off the porch. And oddly enough, she washes all the windows on the first floor.

Now on the third day, Jack Allen sits out on the porch as usual watching the sun set. Theresa comes out of the house. She gives him a hard stare and then she sits down next to him.

In the last few years, having more time on his hands, Jack Allen has taken to rescuing injured animals. There was a small owl smack in the center of the road that wouldn't let him drive by. He got out of his truck and went right up to it. Apparently, it couldn't fly.

Jack Allen got a stick and set it near the owl and the owl climbed right up on it. He took the owl back to the farm and put it in the barn. Figured mice would make a fine owl snack.

Now what is odd, as Theresa sits next to Jack Allen, is that the little owl comes walking out of the barn toward the house. It hops up the stairs onto the porch. It then comes over, jumps up, and sits on the arm of the couch next to Theresa.

And there they sit for an hour after the sun sets—farmer, girl, and owl. Pretty cute I would say. Life has these charming moments.

Theresa also had a thing for Jack Allen's other rescues. A few months back, Jack Allen had spotted a little puppy dog in the ditch next to the road as he drove into town. He stopped, picked it up, and took it home. He lets it run around outside during the day. But at night he keeps it indoors. Not safe at night for a little puppy dog to be on its own.

And there are also three baby raccoons farmer Jack Allen found abandoned in the woods. He took them home. He keeps them in the shed. Feeds them peanuts, bread, apples, and a little dog food.

The thing is that on the fifth day since the girl's arrival Jack Allen would see Theresa cradling the dog or a raccoon in her arms as she walked about yard or house. And she found her own rescues —she made friends with a pheasant and a couple of wild rabbits. They came right up to her. Maybe the owl had spread the world that this was a place of animal hospitality.

On the sixth day, Jack Allen comes down to the kitchen and there on the table is a potted flower called amethyst mist coral bells. And on the windowsill is another plant, a carefully potted— lily-of-the-valley.

Theresa has discovered Jack Allen's tiny flower garden. Besides those two flowers Jack Allen has daylilies, a pretty flower. There are blue and pink Columbines and asters. And there are Ligularia with their tall spires that rise in June and July.

On the seventh day after Theresa arrived, Jack Allen drives into town for some supplies. Turning onto the main road and about a half mile down Jack Allen stops his truck. There in the ditch is a Volkswagen kombi, a little minibus. It has hippie type paintings on the side—a moon, waves breaking, mountains with snow. That sort of thing.

Jack Allen inspects it. Looks like maybe the axle is busted. The girl was lucky she hadn't killed herself. There was also a tree stuck by lightning on the other side of the road. Jack Allen figured with the wind and rain the girl took the wrong turn and, with the lightning striking so close, she lost control.

The next day Jack Allen uses his tractor to pull the kombi out of the ditch. He calls into town and asks if anyone knows how to fix it. Has a friend come out to look at the kombi. The friend tows it away. A few weeks later the kombi is back all fixed, but Theresa by then had decided to stay.

A few days later, Jack Allen notices something odd as he is coming into the house from out back. About eighty feet away from the house the air is slightly warmer. And then if he steps forward a few inches the air is slightly colder. "Humm," he says aloud. He never noticed any unusual phenomena like that with the other girl.

He puts his hand up and sure enough, as he moves his hand closer to the house the air falls in temperature and as he pulls his hand back the air is warmer. He then put his hand right on the spot where the temperature changes and suddenly there is a faint flash of light before his eyes. It is like being on a mountain top and looking out into the blue sky.

But when he looks again nothing happens. But there is a feeling that went with the flash that stays with him. He feels like he weighs five or ten pounds less when he walks toward the house and the weight comes back when he walks out of the house.

Now Jack Allen is not the kind of man who draws quick conclusions when no conclusions need be made. You could say Jack Allen has a judicial temperament. Ambiguity does not bother him and he knows he only needs to decide what something is when

14

there is a practical reason to do so. All the same, Jack Allen is slightly more alert around the girl from now on.

But it takes no special alertness to notice another odd thing. After taking a walk in the woods, Jack Allen comes down the path toward the house and stops. It is late in the afternoon. The light blue of the sky is at the edge of starting to fade. Jack Allen looks at that sky and he sees what he has never seen before. That fading light blue now seems to have twenty different shades.

There is blue violet, cyan, cerulean, light cobalt, a hint of turquoise, steel blue, cornflower, teal, aqua, celeste, maya blue .... The naming was confusing for Jack Allen. But the sight was amazing. He kept staring and asking himself, "Why haven't I ever seen this before?" It was like the sky was a window through which he was gazing into another universe.

Now with Theresa, who still only spoke a few words each week, there came about a change in the evening ritual of sitting on the porch. One night she grabbed one of Jack Allen's feet, takes off his shoe and sock, and gives him a foot massage.

It seems okay to him. It feels fine. It is relaxing. He didn't realize there were so many achy muscles in a foot that were there to awaken at her touch. A day later she massages his other foot.

The following evening she massages his hands. And that is when he saw what she was doing. In touching him, she was linking their two minds together. It was that sense again of standing on top of a mountain and looking off into the blue sky.

In the valley below there were raging storms, lightning, hail, wind shears, and thunder rumbling. The storm was conflict with hot air colliding with cold air, wet with dry, low with high pressure, electric with magnetic, and winds colliding and rolling over each other. The storm was Theresa's soul.

But the sky above was clear, open, vast, unattached, and free of all fear—for Theresa that was farmer Jack Allen's mind. She wanted a piece of it. She wanted their two minds to join.

Farmer Jack Allen says speaking to himself, "I spend morning and evening out here on the porch. Things are quiet and even still, as still as the night sky where the moon and stars appear. I have mind enough to share child. Help yourself. You are welcome to it."

And each night after that when she was not rubbing his foot, his hand, or his shoulders, she would hold his hand as they sat beside each other silently. There was a point in time when nearly a year had past that Jack Allen knew she had gotten what she had come for. He could sense it. Though storms still appeared in her soul, her mind had become like the sky—whether there are storms present or not, the sky remains what it is—open, vast, free, detached, and embracing every change while itself remaining clear.

Late the next day Jack Allen takes Theresa's hand and walks with her a ways toward the covered bridge near the woods. He lets go of her hand. And then he gestures with his own hand toward the open, blue sky above.

Theresa knows what he wants her to do. She stares at that sky and within twenty minute's time clouds have formed and there is a heavy down pour. And then he gestures again with his hand toward the sky. Theresa stares at the sky again and then suddenly the rain stops.

Now you might wonder how farmer Jack Allen came up with the idea that Theresa could control weather like that. But the thing is that when you can go for hours on end without a single thought entering your mind you can see things and think thoughts that you never had before. Insight can come out of nowhere.

Jack Allen just knew that this was a final test, a parting gift, that he was to give Theresa. Like the other girl who once stayed with him for a year, he knew in advance she would soon leave. It was Theresa's time to depart.

A younger man no doubt would have wanted to have his way with Theresa. But with Farmer Jack Allen this having your way thing never came up. Well, that is not exactly true.

The last night before she left, Jack Allen was in a deep, dreamless sleep. Yet even where there are no dreams you can still be alert and notice things going on. But even so you may have a hard time recalling what you observed or experienced when you wake up.

In the morning, taking a shower, half way done, it suddenly came to Jack Allen that this nineteen year old girl had climbed into his bed during the night and had her way with him. How can I describe it? I don't think I can other than to say perhaps it was her way of saying goodbye, or just simply thanking him. Do men really understand women? Or, on the other hand, we could dismiss this event as unsubstantiated speculation and say maybe Jack Allen's imagination was playing tricks on him.

When he comes down the stairs and looks out the window her kombi is gone. But there is a drawing on the table. It is of a little cottage out back behind the house with chimney, kitchen, bathroom, and a porch to sit on.

The message is clear: "If you build it, I will come back."

Six months later the cottage is done. Carpenter, plumber, electrician, roofer, and painter had all finished their jobs. A week later farmer Jack sniffs the air and smells the scent of cedar wood. He looks out back and the light in the cottage is on, smoke is coming out of the chimney, and the kombi is parked to the side. Theresa has returned.

How do you explain a story like this? Farmer Jack Allen might be right to say, "Life's greatest secret is that she is full of surprises and these surprises tend to get thrown in front of your feet if you are already in on the secret."

A sailor sailed off to distant continents seeking his destiny in places new and in seas uncharted. He was driven from within by passion and pride and a thirst for the unknown that he could not define.

His quest came with a price. He left his fair maiden behind. If he had been wiser, he would have found a way to balance his need for love and his desire to sail distant seas.

Over the horizon he voyaged past dangers such as reefs, hidden shoals, great storms, windless weeks, Sargasso seas, starvation, pirates, and disease. The girl he left behind waited for a time. Realizing he was not returning, she found another man to love.

Yet, anchored in a distant island bay in the dead of night, the sound of the wind and waves fades away. And, without external measures to mark the changing hours, time slows and comes to a stop. As our sailor, now a Captain, sits at a table he says to the women as if she has appeared before him in a dream, "I never left you. You have always been here beside me wherever I go. Your heart is forever my home."

And the woman far away across the sea wakes up in her dream. And she speaks in return as she sends a vision to him. She says, "Here. Look through my eyes. See what I see. In the future, we will live an entire life time together. And in that world no sea, mountains, or forest green shall separate us."

And he replies, "Thank you for your gift of love to me."

And she says, "It is most kind of you to accept it."

And from time to time over the next thirty years they sometimes appear together in dreams that they share in common when they both are asleep. As strange as it may sound to our ears, in their dreams they meet each other as those two future lovers where they laugh, play with their children, and love.

The woman and the Captain have discovered a secret few lovers know—that time and space cannot separate those who love with all of their hearts and souls. Or, to restate my case, their inner oneness was so great it was accepted as payment by fate to make a new world that they would create.

THE CARRIER STRIKE GROUP COMMANDER AND THE MERMAID

He was the Commander of a Carrier Strike Group. He had recently been promoted to a 2-star admiral while in that position. The Strike Group had a Nimitz-class aircraft carrier. There were usually at least one cruiser, a destroyer squadron, and 65 to 70 aircraft. Sometimes there were submarines attached and of course always logistics and supply ships.

One day the Commander went down below deck and had a talk with the head of the machine shop on the Carrier. He said, "When I was young I used to race sailboats. And occasionally I still get this urge when the wind is calm and we are not on patrol to revisit those carefree summers. So I would like you to make me a one man sailboat called a Finn, the kind that used to race in the Olympics. I will lower it off the side and take a little sail. Thin wood with fiberglass overlaid should do the trick. I know you can get this done in a few days. By then I will have a sail flown in that will be ready to rig."

Machine shops on an aircraft carrier are not as big as you might think. But they are well equipped so there was no reason not to fulfill the Commander's request. I mean, you do not exactly refuse a Commander of a Navy Battle Group such a small thing, do you?

All the same, the man in charge of the machine shop knew the executive officer would be breathing down his neck over the issue of safety. And he also sensed the Commander wanted a wild ride and would never settle for a sailboat with a solid keel.

Taking out his iPad, he examined the specs of the Finn and other small sailboats. He then says to the Commander, "I will tell you what. How about I made you a Thistle instead? It is slightly larger but more stable. The hull is more sturdy and there is a little more sail area but I am sure you can handle that. I can have it ready by Friday. What do you say?"

The Commanders looks carefully at the picture on the iPad and replies, "See to it."

And so three or four times a year the Commander would take his Thistle and go sailing amid destroyers and frigates with occasionally a submarine patrolling below. He promised the executive officer never to sail more than half a mile away. He had to be within reach if there was an emergency. Then a chopper could pick him up within ten minutes if need be.

What happened next is a little hard to believe. The Commander is sitting dead in the water fixing a batten in the mainsail of his Thistle a half mile off his carrier. Toward the bow, a girl reaches her arms over the side of the sailboat and smiles at the Commander who is, as always, out sailing alone.

The Commander says to the girl, "Now I know you are not a Navy Seal. What are you doing here?"

The mermaid climbs into the boat and immediately her body shape changes into that of a human woman with legs and everything else in the right shape and in the right place.

The girls says, "It is your mind I find irresistible. You have a unique quality that only a few humans possess. You become what you are gazing upon. No doubt that is why you are leading this battle fleet. You see what others do not see and you make decisions that no one will question because they know of your reputation."

"I will give you that," says the Commander. "How can I say this best? Shall I now ask what you are? Is that how this goes?"

The mermaid says, "I am the part of you that you will never know unless I come to you like this and offer you my body and soul."

And so it was that every two instead of three months the Commander found an opportunity to take his Thistle for a sail. And he sailed a little more than a half mile out so as to have a tad more privacy from spying eyes on board his ships. He got to know the girl well for she was the same as any woman in speech and emotional response. Well, there was of course that mermaid enchantment of loving with every fiber of her being and that pure innocence mermaids possess. And of course it goes without saying she had those mermaid siddhis—the clairsentience—of being able to feel what anyone else feels anywhere on earth in any moment.

One day the girl was leaning against the leeward side of the Thistle. And she says to the Commander of the Carrier Strike Group as his hand gently and with great concentration explores the contours of her hip, "There is a woman in San Diego who is about to commit suicide by drowning. I can revive and enter her body after her soul is gone. The two of us can then be together for the rest of your natural life and if you wish beyond."

The Commander is quick in response. He says, "I would like that very much, but there is one problem."

"What is that?" she asks.

He replies, "When I am with you I do not need to be at sea. You are the sea in the form of a woman. I will never meet another woman whose love is so deep. But you are of nature. You have no human needs. You come to me because I have no desire to possess or own you. When we are together like this there is no you or me —only a oneness and this oneness like the sea itself is complete.

"But I am a Commander. I am bound by duty and honor. I understand what you are offering. You are ready to enter another realm far different than your own in order to love me. But your race does not understand loyalty. Loyalty is a commitment to a specific person that offers to support that person in all that he is. It is solid, stable, and it endures. Your love is all-embracing like water and you are always giving but you do not bond.

"I have to work and produce things, think and evaluate, and use all my will to accomplish my plans. And so sometimes I must put love and feelings off to the side in order to do my job. I have missions that involve justice and taking responsibility for insuring certain outcomes in specific time frames.

"You will always be my teacher in regard to love. You and I flow together perfectly as two streams join and are one. But what I am will never be more than a dream to you, even as giving all of myself in every moment out of pure innocence will never be part of my experience."

Genuinely curious now, the girl asks, "When you say 'bond,' tell me more about what that means?"

The commander replies, "Meeting you, becoming one with you, is a life shattering experience for me. But for you sharing as we have done is the normal way you greet others in your own realm.

"For example, you are unable to say to me, 'We have shared some very special moments together and because of this I will always hold you in my heart.' Special moments have no meaning for you because love is always flowing through you. In my world, love is a rare commodity. Some people die without ever tasting it. So when love touches us with such strength and depth, it justifies our having been alive."

She says, "For me, this moment right now contains the past and the future. The past is not gone and the future is not something yet to be. I am always in this moment now."

The commander replies, "And that is why you will not miss me when I am gone. Love is not less for you when I am not with you. Your love is as vast as the sea—and on the open ocean the sea is the same a billion years ago as it is today. It is hard to even discern the four seasons.

"By contrast, my life is very short. I can't afford to make the same mistake twice. The only way I have been able to be with you is by accepting in any moment I may never see or meet with you again. Without that degree of detachment, I would not be able to work or sleep at night. I would completely lose my edge and my clarity of mind. I would be an absolute wreck—unable to function."

She says, "You make love sound so difficult."

He answers, "With some women the enchantment of love is so great they are impossible to love. It is best to forget about them as if the two had never met. The only other alternative is to enter their realm and become one of them. And this I cannot do with you in this life time."

The mermaid realizing that it is time to go says, "How can I say this best? Shall I say farewell? Is that how it goes?"

The Commander quietly gazes at her.

The mermaid says as she looks into his eyes and slowly lowers herself into the sea, "As other mermaids have said to human beings before me, 'If you ever need me in this lifetime or another simply speak my name and I will be there by your side.'"

And then the mermaid is gone. The waves splash against the hull. The sail luffs. The Commander reaches over with his right hand and takes the helm. He trims the mainsail so it catches the wind. And now he steers back to his aircraft carrier where the executive officer, the deck crew, and carrier air wing are waiting his commands.

In times of yore such as in ancient Rome or further back in Greece, nature was too mysterious and diverse for men to feel at ease with its unknown powers or safely interact with its beauty. And so temples were built to celebrate its holy mysteries.

If you wanted to draw near to the sea with its flowing, giving, renewing hope, and endless adaptability, then you might enter the temple of Neptune. If a priest or priestess was worth anything, if you engage in a ritual or festive celebration, you would leave the temple feeling at least for a while that the sea and you had become friends. That vast blue green expanse from horizon to horizon would be alive within you. You would feel your nature is love and that we are in the end all one.

If you wanted to worship the sun with its dazzling light and endless power to imbue the earth with life, then you would enter the temple of Apollo. And there you would be initiated into a great mystery—that in mastering our limitations we shall attain to divine, immortal being while still in human form. Our innermost and true essence is always close to us—within our hearts if we look for it.

Or if you have some great conflict requiring your total will, if you seek self-mastery, or if you are about to go to war, then you enter the temple of Mars. Place a small vial of your blood on the altar. Then pray and meditate. And finally take back the vial and anoint yourself with this blood which now, through the force of your faith and meditation, mixes with the life force of the god. No matter whatever desires and needs may bind you to life, at least for a while you are now ready to give your entire being without distraction to the task or mission to which you are committed.

Mars is like that. It inspires you so you feel the power of the universe is flowing through you. For the sake of your cause, you may end up sacrificing yourself, but your exuberance and inner sense of fulfillment outweigh the needs of your mortal self.

And certainly everyone will at some point wish to visit the temple of Venus. Julius Caesar himself declared his blood line descended from this goddess. War will bring you prestige, honor, and glory. But if you wish to rule an empire or truly lead men so that you capture their imagination and loyalty, Venus will give you an edge. Charisma and personal magnetism are basic foundations of leadership.

All the same, if you enter the temple of Venus, expect the air to be filled with enchantment. Many seek love for its pleasures and bliss. And indeed if you wish to overcome the barriers separating one from another bliss and pleasure are often required in no small measure.

Nonetheless, Venus is the mistress who has mastered ecstasy —to reach beyond the self and become one with another or something greater than you. In love, you transcend life's limitations while simultaneously uniting with its deepest purposes. When you walk out of a temple of Venus after being initiated into its mysteries, you will finally experience body, soul, and mind for the first time in true harmony.

Ancient Rome. Walk down the street and you can feel the city's heartbeat. There are order and brutality. There are men of great power and also always conspiracies. There are hard work, industry, and productivity and also smoldering passions in individuals and raw emotions ready to erupt in the masses.

There is excitement in the air—foreign wars and expanding territories where separate cultures collide. And you can feel hopelessness, misery, oppression, and despair.

In Rome 23 BC, under Imperator Gaius Julius Caesar Augustus, you can walk over to the foot of Capitoline hill in the western end of the Forum Romanum.

If you are sensitive, even before you reach the staircase, you can sense the aura of the temple before you. It is not the enticement and festivity of the Temple of Venus. No, this is as if you are out in nature. It is overcast. There is no wind and it is silent. It is as if time has stopped. Suddenly your memories are more alive than events in the outer world.

You climb the steps toward the columns and the entrance. And you remember your mythology. You think of Orpheus descending into and returning again from Hades, Psyche crossing the River Styx separating life and death, or Odysseus speaking with the shade of his mother who is among the dead.

But the Underworld is not your destination. You are entering a temple. Nonetheless, you are beginning to view your life from a great distance as if you have had to let go of everything you know and have stepped into the unknown.

If you come here nearly any day in the late afternoon, you might see on these steps a woman sitting unmoving or a man holding his head in his hands. Though you may sense anguish, strangely they are not depressed. Rather, they feel a sense of relief. As they climbed the steps whatever distress or sorrow held them has suddenly let go. Here strong emotions wane and detachment takes control.

As you approach the entrance, the air is slightly cooler. You smell the incense from within, perhaps Myrrh, Poppy, or Cypress. The scent carries a mixture of feelings—something dangerous, formidable, and yet also like a trustworthy mentor, like a general who has had a bad day and yet is happy to meet with his advisor.

As we pass through the entrance, you may feel your stomach slightly tighten and a blood pulse in your head. You take a step forward.

And then again it hits you. To enter the Temple of Saturn is like entering the gates of a graveyard—not as one who comes to mourn but as one who is now among the dead.

It is somber. There is little room for regret or sorrow. There is finality and closure. You carry nothing from your life with you. No possessions, no honor, and no fame.

Saturn is time experienced as nightmare. Life is short and the end comes quick. You sense horror, tension, anxiety, and fear, but you are unable to attach an image to these emotions. They are like an invisible mist that surrounds you and follows you everywhere.

The temple now appears gloomy, dark, forbidding, and haunting. There is a sense of belonging nowhere. There is sadness, despair, feeling alone and abandoned. Without support and without a home, you are on your own.

In the pageantry of life with this mood weighing upon you, you feel you have a small part to play and nothing you do makes any difference. The station you have in life is of no consequence. The five senses offer no real stimulation. The feelings you share with others contain no celebration. For all the freedom you have or do not have, you might as well be living in a jail cell for all the difference it makes.

Ah, Mamercus, a priest I know, comes to greet us. He is from an aristocratic family named Bassianus. For some reason, he is incredibly relaxed. He walks as if he is strolling alongside a stream out in the woods. We enter a small room with an altar and candles. There is a vase in the center filled with water.

We sit down and he begins chanting. The sounds are hypnotic and spellbinding. But it is not a chant as much as a song. It recapitulates our experiences with life from the point of view of Saturn. This Saturn priest is a bard and he is singing a song of what it is to be alive.

Mamercus could be intoning a chorus of a play in a Roman theater except we are on the stage and it is our lives on display. The priest says, "It is not as you think. Time can be a friend. You begin life. You are given gifts. It is how you use what you have been given that counts.

"Saturn only asks that you find in life something of great value to work at or to accomplish. This can be inside yourself or in the outer world. Make something that endures.

"Rome itself is part of this struggle. There are buildings that we build that shall stand for thousands of years. What emperor can enter this city made of stone and leave it filled with marble? What general can set aside his rank and power and return to his villa leaving behind a tradition of honor that shall inspire men down through the ages?

"Each of us is a part of two worlds—an outer world and inner, spiritual world. We live and operate equally in both, even though the outer world seems solid and real and the inner, the spiritual world, feels like a dream.

"You will know when you have entered Saturn's dreams. There are soul to soul and heart to heart connections. What is within others transforms you and you in turn pass on a flame of inspiration to others.

"And yet there is more. Saturn itself can become your spirit guide. In this case, you are not on a spiritual quest. You are not operating as part of some mythic journey of some great hero.

"No. Saturn sets before you work to accomplish on earth that shall endure through all ages of the world and be of value to all races and people.

"You will know when you have undergone the initiation of Saturn. You perceive all men are your brothers and sisters. You see all nations as one community of humanity. And what you do in each moment would and will be honored as a work of the body, heart, and spirit whether it is witnessed thousands of years ago or thousands of years in the future. The words you speak are truth and illuminate like the sun.

"And yet this is not so far away, is it? Who among us has not shined like the sun and the moon to others in a dark night of their lives? To meet others where they are, to be with them and to comfort them, and then to walk by their sides to a place of freedom and light—is this not the greatest and most sacred celebration of life?

"We are here on earth to learn, to grow, to experience new things, and to transform into something more than what we now are.

"And yet Saturn stalks us demanding what even the greatest of world teachers are hard pressed to achieve—

"To demonstrate that we have learned all that can be learned from life in the worlds of form we must show that we are able to create love where love does not exist and that we are able to free in our hearts under the worst and most difficult conditions of life.

"The voice of Saturn says to each of us, 'Learn to be as me— weep not when death and fate take away. Renounce regret, sorrow, and loss. Every ending, separation, farewell, and goodbye is a sacred rite in my eyes. It contains my blessing and my voice.'"

For a little while we sit in silence allowing the words of the priest to echo through our memories and to clarify our choices.

And now our time with Mamercus comes to an end. It is ten o'clock at night. We walk out from among the columns of the Temple of Saturn in ancient Rome. We return to our hovel where the rats occasionally jump up on the table; or else perhaps to our villa on the hill where we sit by the fountain out back in the garden where there is running water and statues made from marble.

In both cases, we know that the life we now live is but a cloak we have put on. We shall take it off and put it on again many times in many different lands and we shall play roles in many different societies; until at last we master the lessons of the physical world and ascend. And then we shall sit in a circle among divine beings that hold in their hands the powers of creation. At which point, Saturn will have accomplished its mission—to insure we attain absolute freedom.

James O'Brien slept as if he was dead. But he should sleep that way for he was quite dead. Funeral was done and casket was six feet down in consecrated ground. He might have thought that resurrection day would be his next stop if Christian doctrine had its firm hands on the helm. Then again, sometimes there are winds that blow us off course.

Oh, it was not that James was uncomfortable or claustrophobic though most would agree it was a tight fit for him in that coffin. He was surrounded by the good earth and he felt at peace. After all, we have heard people say, "final resting place" and "rest in peace." Death provides closure for life's uncertainties. But as others have said, "When things end there are new beginnings."

The tombstone above James on the graveyard grounds read,

James O'Brien
1895-1960

And that should have been the end of it. But this is where our story begins. Now some visitors complained that the cemetery management was not tending the grounds as it should. But management had troubles. There was the scam with annuities that had taken out large chunks of the financial reserves of cemeteries across the country. This cemetery was no exception. But still, the roads remained paved and the trees and shrubs trimmed. Not that it mattered much for James. No one came around anymore with flowers, with tears to shed, or to speak his name aloud.

It happened like this. One fine day James woke up though he should have been fast asleep dreaming the dreams of the dead. First, James sensed the ground around him. He sensed the other coffins in the graveyard. As far as he could tell, he was the only one hanging around. Everyone else must have gone into the light or else abandoned their bones when they let go of their lives.

It took a week or so before James thought of actually doing anything with himself. It was okay with him to let things just be. The thing is, time did not work for James the way he remembered it when he was alive. He noticed this when he saw someone walking through the graveyard. In his mind James could slow that person's movements down. The person then walked oh so slow. Like each step took a minute or more. And James could even bring the person to a stop. One foot raised as the person leaned slightly forward and was about to put his weight on it.

And James could do the opposite. He could speed things up so that forty people seemed to be racing about—an entire week of visitors could come and go in a few moments. But James took this ability to stretch and to shrink time in stride. He realized his mind was out of phase with the normal cycle of day and night. It took him a while to shift gears so that his mind moved at the same speed as the living.

What happened next is that James stood up. Well, he was still underground since he was less than six feet tall. But the top of his head was near the roots of the grass. He could tell that. And he had a sense that if he could get this far he could probably go anywhere he wanted to.

He put that idea to the test. He eased himself out of the ground and sat down. He then looked at his gravestone. Everything seemed in order there. He looked about. No one was in the cemetery though of course there were birds and a few squirrels running around. He sat and watched the animals, the wind in the trees, the grass, flowers, and the clouds until the sun went down.

Next morning James watched the sun come up. It was on toward breakfast time when James sensed that food was not one of those things you need to be concerned with when you are dead. James went for a walk. He strolled over to the gate of the cemetery to see if he could leave the consecrated grounds. He cautiously put one foot down outside the gate. Nothing happened. He walked a few feet farther and looked around again and then walked on.

A few blocks down there were residential homes. James walked on the sidewalk. The body he wore was actually a younger version of himself before the time when he died. Apparently when you are dead you can change your appearance if you want.

James came to a house and went up to the door. He tried knocking just to be polite but there was no sound. He walked through the door into the house. Mildred, the lady of the house, was cleaning a few dishes having just finished breakfast. And that is when James made his first big discovery of the day.

James could see a fog like haze around Mildred. And all of Mildred's memories were like pictures floating in this haze or let us say in Mildred's aura. And as strange as it seemed, James could pick any one of those pictures and enter it and live that memory, as if it was his own experience. But she herself did not know how to do this. Though Mildred was still alive and James was very dead, James felt it odd that the living should act as if they already have one foot in the grave. They forget that the past lives on and is not something that dies and then is buried in the ground.

But there was more. James could sense everyone who had ever loved Mildred. And he could sense the desires, needs, and wants that caused Mildred to make choices and to act. And those choices and acts defined who she had been, who she is, and what she will become.

James walked out of the house going through the wall, then through the fence, and finally through the wall into the next house. James thought to himself, "When you are dead, boundaries do not count for much."

The cat mellowed when he saw James enter and ran off and hid under the bed. But Howard Davis who lived in the house did not notice anything. It was not as if James brought with him a foul smell. Though if someone was present with a psychic nose he might have noticed a scent in the air of the next world and a slight drop in temperature toward cold.

James saw pictures in the aura of Howard too. These pictures were of events that occurred when Howard was stationed in islands off Japan during the last days of World War II. A destroyer was hit by a kamikaze and sank. Barrels of coffee from the sunken ship rolled in on the waves at the beach. Howard salvaged them. Coffee was passed on to his commanding officer who appreciated having it not realizing the tragic source.

James went inside of one of those pictures in the air around Howard. He watched as Howard drank hot coffee he had brewed in the mess hall back during the war. Howard was thinking, as he sipped from the warm cup in his hands, that it was good to be alive. It was good to have survived. A cup of coffee can enable you to step out of time if only by a micro second or two in order to savor the present moment.

There were pictures too of Howard when he was fifty feet down the beach from where General McArthur stepped ashore finally returning to the Philippines; pictures of Howard's daughter in the hospital shortly after being born; pictures of an empty house after his wife had died. There were pictures some bright, some dim; pictures and memories were mostly what were left to him.

And that is when James saw it. Perhaps this "seeing" is why he had awoken when others fell into dreamless sleep or moved on to some faraway place on the Other Side. This was something James had left undone when he was still alive. Something he had to finish up before moving on or before his next step, whatever it was.

James insight came from Mildred and Howard. Mildred was not her husband or her children and yet having them in her life made her Mildred. And Howard was not a man who lived a healthy life. The war drained him of his desire to share his experiences of the past or to pursue new experiences in the future.

And with an effort James could recall his own life that was no more, gone, left behind. He too had pictures, though now they were fading since no one was shining any light in their direction for quite some time.

But James saw that the good earth has always been here. The seed that sleeps in the ground awakens in spring, rises up, grows, and becomes the tree that itself releases seeds on the wind. Animals hunt, they eat, and they mate. They live and experience their five senses according to their individual nature.

Humans perhaps have a little more intelligence than animals. People can awaken in their dreams or dream while awake. They can envision and make plans that bring new things into being.

"Is that what I am to supposed to see?" James asks himself. "The limitations with which I lived never defined who I was. I am not the product of my past. You can wake up anytime, look around, uplift your mind, or step out of the ground. Had I only known you can step inside of another's soul and live the other's life as if it is your own."

But insight comes when it does. The good earth nurtures us. It gives rest and peace and it also grants new beginnings. Maybe the bones have a final resting place but not the soul. It journeys on.

"Step free!" James shouts out though no one hears his words.

James leaves Howard's house and, as he continues on down the sidewalk, he says, "I think I will follow this street. Perhaps I will meet some others who are walking around like me."

It was a dark time
He was a knight who fought for the light
Without knowing
If his acts were wrong or right
He met a mermaid one day
Along the shore by a lake

B eing both battle-hardened and widely traveled, he had the skill of a merchant. He could tell how much a man wanted something by the way he looked at an item.

He could read in another's face if horror or wonder had touched him, and if these things were small or great.

He could tell by others' breath and the movement of their chests whether they had lived in peace or suffered distress.

He could tell by gazing into another's eyes how well they had lived their lives—if there was waste or if they had been guided by someone wise.

He could tell by listening to another's voice—even hearing only one or two words spoken aloud—if their lives were lived with honor or if their lives were shaped by a mistake.

So when he met the mermaid in the form of a woman he noticed right away what most others would have missed. She is like water, changing her form and shaping her responses in a new and unique way as each moment unfolds and with each person she is with.

Knowing that some opportunities occur only once in a life time, the knight seizes the moment and asks her, "How do I become what you are?"

The mermaid says, "You do not ask, 'How do I love you?' but instead you ask, 'How do I become what you are?'

"All other men seek to possess nature—to master it, to control it, and to turn it to a productive end. Only a few of your race have come this far—to open your heart to embrace rather than to take."

"You must already know the wisdom of nature. Gaze on the sea contemplating the images, sounds, smells, taste, and touch of water. Then open your heart to feel what is underneath the outer form.

"Here there is a love that encircles the planet and seeks to nurture every creature. Become this love and then you shall be as I am—one who gives all of oneself in every moment and for whom love is never lost."

The knight replies, "It is not enough to have the words. You speak of things the mind by itself can never find."

The mermaid answers, "This is why you must remain completely alert and perceive without any thoughts intervening even as you have been doing from the first moment you began speaking to me."

The knight asks, "Can you show me the way?"

She says, "Take my hand." And this he does.

She goes on, "Now you feel what is inside me—I am water in human form. To touch me is to feel the winds caressing the waves on and on without end. There is no identity—the beauty of the sea is what I am—the waves running free, the silent depths, every manner of creature, and the purity of receptivity that can find the beauty and wonder of the stars shining within its heart.

"The waterfall—to let go and to fall into the embrace of air and space; the lake with its mirror-like stillness—the beauty of the universe shines from its face; the river and the stream that bring to life whatever is near; the mist, the fog, the cloud, the rain—I am forever free—every form I can take and yet I am always the same. The definition of my very being is seen in the act of giving.

"If you can look upon nature as you look upon me, if you can in your heart unite with that beauty even as your body can become one with mine, then this I promise you—the two of us will be forever joined."

The knight says, "Now I understand. You are myself in another form. How could I not have seen this before? Love designs each moment of time. As a knight, I now see my task—to serve her purposes and to fight on her behalf."

The Oracle is in a little cave in Bali, not too far from Denpasar International Airport. You can rent a car and drive to the rocky peninsula of Uluwatu. From there you will probably need to hire a local guide. Not too many guides will take you there so ask for Putu. He is happy to assist as long as you pay in cash, preferably U.S. dollars.

Now Alessio was a mob boss who ran an operation in the United States. He had heard about the oracle in a roundabout way. One of his captains had a daughter. And this daughter had a friend who liked to wander all over the Far East, often by herself. And as she wandered, she discovered she had a gift for running into gurus, mystics, and wise men.

Even walking down the street in Mumbai or Kolkata, an enthusiastic male would approach her and say, "You must meet my guru." And she would go with him and his guru would be delighted to make her acquaintance. In fact, the guru would offer to teach her things he had never taught any of his own disciples.

Well, the captain could hardly resist describing this wacko, spaced out New Age girl who wanders about. He told Alessio how he had met her one day when he had lunch with his daughter. The girl came strolling in wearing a thin sari and sat down at the table.

The captain told Alessio that one of her stories was about entering a mystical cave in Bali called the Oracle. The cave was only known to a few of the local people. But the girl claimed the Oracle had all knowledge and was in fact a continuation of the Oracle of Delphi in Ancient Greece with a few enhancements.

Now Alessio liked to collect rare things. For example, he had some valuable paintings some of which were well-known. And he also had some paintings in a private collection that he had to keep hidden from the public eye. You cannot put these on the open market to be bought or sold.

And every now and then Alessio liked to indulge a wild, crazy whim. Something would capture his attention. And then he would go off and experience something new that most people could not imagine.

Alessio knew a little secret about life. You are as young as you feel and feeling young, as he would say with his thick Italian accent which he rarely used, "It is all about spontaneity—there are things you can make happen; there are things you can make not happen; and then there are things that happen on their own but only if you let them."

So Alessio decided to go see this cave. First of course he had to entice the pretty young New Age thing to divulge the cave's location. But being a master of charm and persuasion, as well as numerous devious methods, he easily extracted from her the information he desired.

Apparently her flair for running into masters and gurus sometimes included masters from the dark side. But she did not judge. She knew that some people you have to respect and some people it is best to stay as far away from as possible.

Not knowing anything about Alessio, she asked him straight out, "Why exactly do you want to go to this cave?" And the boss replied honesty, "I wish to ask the Oracle what is missing from my life. After all, this question can only be asked by a middle aged man like myself who senses there is something very important in life that he has not yet encountered."

His tone of voice and explanation were more than convincing. She knew he was not lying.

He flew out a week later and rented a car and found a guide as she had suggested. And now he walks into the cave. There are candles with matches just inside the front entrance. He lights a candle and walks on maybe for a quarter of a mile into the darkness.

There he finds a little sign that says in both Balinese and Indonesian, "Put out the candle. Make your case, ask your question, or state your doubt." The girl had already translated the words for Alessio so he knew what it said.

He put out the candle and then, addressing the darkness, he says, "I have seen much in my life. I know what motivates men. I know when the law is useful and I know when the law is no longer your friend. I watch over my community. I am a patron of the arts. I support the Church. I care for my family. I adhere to tradition and I can also sense when tradition must give way to change so that there can be a new beginning. I do what I love and I do it well.

"Yet in all that I observe—of what makes me and others feel alive—the essence of life remains hidden. I know in my bones that there are special things have not yet been revealed to me."

And a voice from the darkness and silence asks, "What do you see right now around you?"

And Alessio replies, "I see nothing at all. Everything is cloaked in darkness, for you had me put the candle out."

The voice asks, "What has been your deepest motivation?"

And the Alessio replies, "To escape poverty and assist others to do the same."

And the voice then asks, "What is your highest inspiration?"

Alessio answers, "What inspired me most was when don Agostino, with complete calmness and confidence, spoke to his men about his plan to bring an end to a problem he had. It was beautiful. He was precise like a diamond cutter cutting a diamond and also wild and noble like a lion that has broken free of its cage. That was pure inspiration in my eyes."

The voice asks, "What has been your greatest desire that you have satisfied?"

And Alessio says, "Taking a woman in such a way that every cell in her body is responding to me."

And the voice asks, "What is the greatest dream you have not yet fulfilled?"

Alessio answers, "I want not only to command respect from those who know and work with me. I want them to feel deep down that it has been a pleasure and an honor for them to have known me.

And the voice asks, "What was the worst way you have betrayed yourself?"

Alessio says, "I was mean to my friends when I was a teenager. If they were not loyal to me, I settled the score. I did not need to take things so far."

And the Oracle asks, "What is the best that has happened to you so far in this life?"

And Alessio replies, "For the first ten years of my profession, I worked my ass off just to survive. The second ten years, I had my head above water but there were still times when the outcome of my decisions were iffy.

"But in the last ten years the best things have been happening almost without effort. I have stayed on top of technology. The legal system assists me. There is no longer a need for violence because there are now countless ways to persuade others to work with me rather than oppose me. And more markets are opening for my services than I can possibly handle. This has been the best—accomplishing more with less effort than I could ever have imagined."

And the Oracle asks, "If there was a gift you wished life had given you at the beginning, what would that be?"

And the don says, "A few—just a few whose love and trust were never withdrawn or in doubt."

The Oracle goes on, "I am rarely asked this question, 'What is the essence of life that is hidden?' It is not for nothing I speak from out of darkness and silence.

"In each of your answers, your motivation, inspiration, desire, satisfaction, what you dream, the worst that has happened, the best, and the gift you wished to have had, and all that it is to feel alive reduce to four feelings—electrifying enthusiasm and conviction, pure innocence and love that is endless in its giving, the thrill and wonder of mastering the unknown, and the quiet ecstasy of accomplishing all you have set before yourself—these four flow in and through each other.

"They are the essence of life—every situation of conflict and desire, dream and longing, inspiration and threat has existed to enable you to experience and to embody them.

"But these four arise from what is inside of me—I am so open and empty every person and situation in life is a part of me. I was there when out of hatred you put an end to your friends. Though you were not listening, I was telling you there is another way; the pain inside you only exists because of your attachment to an illusion.

"I was there when you saw don Agostino solve his problem. I was speaking to you, 'Celebrate the strength in a man. But understand a greater strength can be found inside you like the endurance of mountains, like the brilliant and dynamic action of lightning, and like the wild exhilaration of the wind.'"

"And with lifelong friends who love and give but who never appeared, I was saying to you from the beginning, 'Give to others the very thing you wish to have for yourself. Then life will find in you a man who is worthy to fulfill its deepest plans.'"

Alessio says, "Let me see if I understand what you are saying. I get all that about the electrifying conviction, innocence of love, sheer bliss in taking hold of and claiming the unknown, and getting things done and the satisfaction that ensues. But are you telling me that you—the Oracle—are the essence of what it is to feel fully alive?"

And here Alessio pauses a bit and waits in silence. And then he goes on, "In other words, if I understand this right, the way to be fully alive is to give to others opportunities to experience new things and also to assist them, more than assist, at times guarantee that their lives are all they can be. Is my summary correct?"

The Oracles says, "Your original question as you stated it to the young lady who once visited me was—'What is missing from my life?'

43

"What is missing from your life is a feeling of being one with every living being. You notice the silence that surrounds both of us. If I pause from speaking, it is here, everywhere, all inclusive. Like this silence, I am totally receptive without judgment or evaluation. And yet, I point out what you already know and have experienced. I am your own conscience recalling, reflecting, and contemplating what is yet to be done.

"You have arrived at a point in life few men ever encounter. You are indeed able to think others' thoughts, feel others' feelings, and assist them in fulfilling their needs and dreams.

"In your tradition it is said, 'Know your friends, but know your enemies better.' You are a man who is capable of being everyone's friend. You are able to sense and to assist others in discovering for themselves what makes them feel most alive. This is why you have entered this place of darkness and silence.

To meet your better self who has been waiting all these years to make your acquaintance."

And Alessio, the mafia boss, went home. And he became a better man.

A sorcerer in Tibet has the power to kill others with his magic. As his arrogance grows, the sorcerer announces that he plans to kill a humble Tibetan priest who lives nearby.

The Tibetan priest has a practice of meditating on Prajnaparamita (which is known as the perfection of wisdom and is sometimes visualized in the form of a goddess who is the mother of all enlightened beings).

His meditation goes like this:

> Relax. Take a breath. Allow your consciousness to become a vast, empty space of pure nothingness. Here there is no form, no center, no circumference, no body, no thoughts, only pure awareness that has no need to refer to anything in order to sustain or define itself.
>
> And since there are no boundaries and no form, there is no separation. And without separation, only oneness exists. You can recall experiences and review actions. Yet, in this state of mind, anything that separates one from another dissolves.

To put this simply: There is no enemy present. There is no attack occurring. There is no one to attack and nothing to attack with.

And so it was that the evil magician unleashes the full power of his magic against the priest. This is the power to destroy, annihilate, and obliterate.

Martial artists spend a life time developing their ability to focus energy through their body and mind to overcome or defeat an opponent. Magicians sometimes train in this way as well. It is about survival. But to avoid abuse when directing such force, it is best to proceed in harmony with the laws of the universe.

And so our malicious, evil sorcerer sends out a massive amount of will and power against the Tibetan priest. But alas, the energy that is sent cannot find anyone to attack. It looks here. It looks there and everywhere, but there is no priest anywhere to be found. The priest has become like a mirror that reflects the void.

A torpedo launched from a submarine containing its own sonar goes looking for its target. But if it cannot find the target the torpedo returns to its source—the only thing around that is available to attack. The black magician falls dead. He is a victim of the magical attack unleashed by his own will.

The void meditation practiced by the priest dissolves evil because evil, in order to function, requires something it can possess, control, or destroy. But in the void there are none of these things. Still, individuals have the right to learn from the consequences of their actions. You cannot take away freedom of choice. But through uniting with the void you can limit a malicious will so it harms only itself.

Once a young woman was abandoned by her lover. She left her village in shame when she discovered she was pregnant. She knew that for the rest of her life she and her child would be social outcasts. So she went off into the woods to die. But there, in the middle of the night, she met the goddess Dawn who appeared and walked by her side.

The goddess Dawn said to her, "If you will put aside your despair and have faith in the light, I will give you a child like no other who has ever walked upon the earth. He shall be called Lugnas, for he will be a child of the sun."

And then the goddess gave her a bird to keep her company as a sign that dawn follows the night. The woman kept the child and her life. She learned that even during the greatest anguish and abandonment you can still sing from the depths of your heart. Even in a place and time of great darkness, beauty still reigns triumphant and marvelous.

And because of her faith, she did not become numb; she did not deny or repress her loss. The women cast off her despair, took heart, and returned to her village. Since she was already three months pregnant, she bore a son six months later.

As her child grew up, the mother discovered that he indeed had special gifts. The birds sang at night wherever he was. But the power of the blessing he carried with him was this: people forgot their anger, greed, and conflicts and made peace with each other when he was around.

His presence brought the world into focus. Suddenly, without explanation, people could see their best courses of action no matter how great the confusion. They felt they had taken a drug that makes you euphoric and fills you with inspiration. Such was the power of peace that walked with him.

When he was near, no one, no matter how cold, callous, or cruel, could think, feel, or imagine doing anything unkind or evil. For once in their lives, they felt so happy they could dance and be friendly even with their worst enemies. The priests in that land who were high initiates said of Lugnas, "A Guardian of one of the planetary spheres has come down to guide and to watch over him."

When Lugnas was around, the air was clearer. Instead of being able to see islands fifty miles off in the sea, those standing on shore could see islands two hundred miles away as if they were next door. And there were other phenomena too—activities that were normally annoying and irritating become playful and humorous. Frustration switched to delight. The worst and darkest secrets were understood for what they were and left behind.

And enemies who turned into friends? It was like this: the one you hate the most suddenly becomes a mirror that reflects back to you the path and the means for attaining your deepest dreams. And so it was that people put aside their arts of war and began celebrating the new friends they had miraculously found.

Of course, there was a discordant note sounding amid the harmony of peace making and acquiring new friends. Some individuals refused to be ensorcelled so easily. They felt as if something important in life had been taken from them. But what they had lost was only their greed and fear. All the same, the darkness in their past would reappear in bits and pieces of bad dreams that remained with them when they awoke in the morning.

Was Lugnas taking away their free will? Or was he granting opportunities to feel in new ways? When you are around someone with great power and a loving heart, you discover your own mistakes and errors right at the start. When the light is so bright, it is hard to deny that the darkness inside you is of your own making.

Lugnas' career as a peacemaker started when a woman grew tired of having her sons killed one after the other in a longstanding feud between her clan and another. She called Lugnas to come and help. She thought that grace and blessing must follow a man for whom the birds sing from dust to dawn.

And sure enough, when Lugnas took up residence in the village, the next morning the rival clans were out fixing fences together and digging wells. And later in the evening, they were buying each other drinks in the pub. After this success, Lugnas decided to walk around the kingdom visiting all the villages where there were strife and dire conflicts. When you find your niche—something you are good at—it is a pleasure to pursue it.

His miraculous powers to bring peace were so predictable and consistent that Lugnas came to be regarded as a force of nature, like lightning, winter, or spring—something you cannot resist; you just have to accept it. His reputation grew so strong that when people heard he was coming, on their own initiative, they put aside their differences and make peace.

In which case, they sent Lugnas a messenger who showed him a written agreement. They agreed to live in harmony for an entire year. The rival factions or enemies would avoid strife in any form. And as collateral, they sent him gold or jewels to hold in safekeeping, to be turned over to the poor should they fail to keep their promise.

They knew that if he heard they were bickering, it was as likely as not that he would come calling. They would then be so struck by peace they would end up moving in with their enemies and treating them as long lost friends. But this result was too embarrassing to contemplate. Even enemies could find common ground and work together to avoid an outcome that traded pride and strife for humility and a new way of life.

Now I am sure that you can imagine that eventually someone would contrive a means to oppose Lugnas. Sure enough, two villages had a feud that had been going on for as long as anyone could remember—kind of like in modern times when clans or tribes of the same country have hated each other more than they hate foreign invaders.

And Lugnas, they found out, was on his way. A merchant, who offered gossip along with his wares, made a hobby of keeping track of Lugnas' affairs. And this merchant informed the local communities.

The two sets of village elders took heed of these rumors and reviewed the testimony concerning Lugnas from credible witnesses. The two opposing factions then conceived a plan to avoid this strange dawning of peace. They had always fought each other and they hoped to continue until one or the other clan was finally annihilated. For some, carrying on a feud is a matter of honor.

And so, not wishing to have their traditions violated by a will not of their own making, the people in both villages agreed to leave in mass before Lugnas arrived. They moved up into the surrounding hills. But Lugnas still came. He settled casually into one of the houses as if it had his name written on the door.

A few nights passed and then a few weeks. But the people knew Lugnas was still around because the birds kept singing all night. So they decided to send a spy to find out exactly what he was doing. But no one was willing to go. They were too afraid of Lugnas. Just listening to the stories about him made some of them sick to their stomach for days.

But at last a blacksmith with a strong stomach said he would go and see for himself if the rumors were true or not. He crept down to the valley before dawn. He took a position just outside the village though he felt terribly uncomfortable with all the birds singing in the trees above him.

When the blacksmith returned three days later, his report was very bad. He said that he had witnessed firsthand the appearance of a great being of light, a vast angelic power in the form of a huge man. This spirit descended from the sky, leaping down on top of the house where Lugnas was staying. And then it climbed right inside through the roof. It stayed all night and left again at dawn.

The people from the two villages came together in a little valley up in the hills to discuss the situation. For the second time, they were in complete agreement—all of them refused to surrender to the saint's power.

This left them little alternative. They would have to stay up in the hills adding rooms to shepherd's' huts, making the most of sheep herding, gathering wild berries, and such. For them it was a small price to pay for freedom—these people were vehement about their independence and their right to determine their own destinies.

An entire year went by. Lugnas was still living down in one or another of their old villages. But they just took it in stride and settled in where they were. Out of necessity, they formed a new village where they could meet together and pool their resources to better survive the common calamity that had befallen them.

They were like a couple recently divorced and who were done dividing their assets. But now, impoverished, they still get together over a drink to complain about the cost of their attorneys and the rotten way things had turned out. For some, finding fault with the world will always be a favorite pastime.

Years passed by. The people never went back to their old villages. They were too terrified of Lugnas even though he had long since left them to their own devices. They thought his presence had contaminated their entire valley with dreams of peace. And to add insult to injury, the birds would start singing to greet the morning round about midnight.

So they stayed up in those hills enjoying their poverty, their solitude, and their freedom. As far as they were concerned, the fact that they no longer brawled or killed each other was altogether beside the point. And from time to time when someone married a member of the other clan? That was all right. It was a way of strengthening their collective will to fight the light—that is, the injustice when someone else tells you what is right or how to live your life.

PART II

DREAMS II

A man of questionable character met Buddha walking down the road. And recognizing the Buddha, he confronts him demanding Buddha respond to his question, "What possible thing could you say to me that would make the slightest difference in the way I live my life?"

And Buddha replies, "If you could see yourself in this moment through my eyes you would attain perfect enlightenment."

And the man says, "Sir, your words have no meaning. Can you say it in a different way?"

So Buddha replies, "What I dream becomes reality, for my mind is boundless light.

"When I sense the faintest beginning of desire, I already experience every satisfaction possible, for my bliss is endless.

"And when I perceive another with a problem or amid a conflict, I see the path that individual will follow where every problem is solved and every conflict resolved, for the harmony in which I exist is infinite.

"Your every memory I experience in this moment as if it is my own. You are me and I am you in another form."

And the man asks, "Is this why they say you are the god of compassion?"

And Buddha replies, "It has been said that I will continue to incarnate to assist human beings as long as suffering exists on earth. Some call this compassion. But in reality I experience each person as being part of myself. To be me is to experience love in which there is no separation."

And the man sees that the person he had been no longer exists. He is gone.

And after this when he looked into another person's eyes he understood there is no separation, for like Buddha, the other person's life felt as if it was his own life in another form.

Buddha was walking down a road one day and a woman was walking toward him. And when they came face to face the Buddha bows down before the woman and says, "Ah, a mermaid. What a delight!"

And the mermaid replies, "Of all men I have ever met, you are the only one who recognizes who I am."

The Buddha says, "It is understandable that no one sees who you are. Human beings do not know what love is much less do they perceive spirits from other realms who dwell among them. But you are not just loving, are you? You are love itself wearing a woman's body.

"Unlike you, humans do not sense that they are surrounded by a sea of love. And so they do not know how to let that endless love flow through them in every moment of time. This is why they are attached to their egos and constantly take more than they give. They are all burning up like a candle using up its wax. They have not yet united to nature from inside."

The woman says, "There is something you not telling me. What is it?"

Buddha replies, "The truth is you are asking me for knowledge that does not belong to your race. And this you are doing only because you are standing here within my aura and so beginning to perceive as I perceive."

And the mermaid says, "Is not my love richer, more natural and spontaneous, and more giving than your own?"

Buddha replies, "I have not chosen during this life to embody within myself the energy of the realm of nature from which you have come. I am compassionate but I do not love as you love. No one who touches my body would say from the sensation in their fingertips that they are touching the sea."

And putting forth his hand he grasps the girl's upper arms and says, "But in touching you it is not a human woman with a personality and human identity I am touching. I am touching the sea itself. Your love is inexhaustible because in every moment the love of the sea flows through you."

"And so why do I feel incomplete for the first time in my life as I talk to you?" She asks.

And the Buddha replies, "You could place me anywhere in this galaxy among any race of sentient beings and I would remain with them, assisting and inspiring them, until that race ascends and attains enlightenment and absolute freedom.

And indeed if you were on any other planet where there is a sea you would continue to be exactly who you are—love itself, forever innocent, forever free, giving all of yourself in every moment without hesitation or limitation. But you need that sea with its inner energy of love to flow through you to accomplish these things."

"And so the difference?" asks the girl.

The Buddha replies, "The difference is that I create love. I need no sea. The love within me is united to infinity."

And the girl asks, "What would I be if I needed no sea to love and yet when someone touched me they still felt the sea? I would no longer be a mermaid, would I?"

"No," says the Buddha. "You would no longer be a mermaid. You would be the perfection of love."

"Ah," says the girl. "I now understand why you have been holding back. Some things one must first find within one's own heart before a path opens up. But are there any other mermaids who have chosen to follow such a path?"

"Yes," replies the Buddha. "The mermaid queen Istiphul, in her innermost dreams, seeks to become the perfection of love, the highest expression of love that exists on this planet."

The girl says gazing upon the Buddha, "I see your aura clearly. I see all your chakras as they once were and now are. I see how you have united yourself to formless awareness and so have attained absolute freedom.

"But I also see a dream deep within you—that one day this entire race shall ascend and attain perfect enlightenment. But yet there is more. They shall also fulfill the dream within the heart of the earth itself and become one with the universe. The sea of love that they shall finally become shall have no shores. The winds that drive its waves shall create bliss and in its depths there is an ecstasy that shines brighter than the stars."

"Of all those who dwell on earth," says the Buddha, "you alone see me for who and what I am."

"Tell me more about the perfection of love," says the girl as the two of them walk side by side down the road.

This story takes place in an alternate reality—another world than ours where different choices were made.

One day Buddha is walking down the road and he meets a great warrior. This is not just any great warrior. This man is a military genius of the caliber of Alexander the Great. It would have been easy for him to conquer not only India, but also Japan, Korea, China, Mongolia, and even spread his empire to encircle most of the Mediterranean Sea. As warriors go, he is the best of the best.

Seeing the Buddha, he walks right up to him and says without the slightest hesitation or doubt, "Great master, I have sought to master myself and I have accomplished much through my efforts. And yet satisfaction eludes me.

"Furthermore, I know that if I put forth my will I can conquer the known world and more. I have this special ability. I can communicate soul to soul and heart to heart with others a certain amount of my own power and will. My generals are nearly as wise as me and my soldiers are indomitable in battle. No army can defeat them.

"And yet I feel as if all I can do would still be in vain. What glory would it be to conquer the world if I cannot defeat war itself? For after I am gone, no matter how great my empire and the leaders I leave behind, fighting will break out. Wars will again be fought. And all that I have accomplished will fade like grass that withers and is then replaced by new sprouts.

"I see in you kindness, generosity, and compassion—you are willing to answer any honest and sincere inquiry put to you. Therefore, answer my question. Demonstrate to me now and to the world that shall be hereafter that there is wisdom so vast, deep, and profound that it can end war forever by following your directions."

And the Buddha replies, "Any opponent you face has a mind like your own. All you need do to end war forever is to join your mind with the mind of your opponent so the two of you become as one living being working together to fulfill each other's dreams. Accomplish this and teach it to others and then wars shall be no more."

And the warrior asks, "How can this be? Two men striving against each other with all their might and power—each seeking to dominate and to master the other? Join their minds and you will have chaos, a nightmare like a firestorm and a whirlwind meeting. The result is a conflagration."

And Buddha replies, "To join your mind to another's mind requires but one thing—perfect, mirror like clarity, even as now in this moment I am joining my mind to yours."

The warrior asks, "How can this be taught?"

Buddha replies, "If you gaze upon a seed, you can sense the past, present, and future of the seed and of the tree it is to become: the seed is carried by wind or falls as part of a fruit. It sinks into the soil and merges with the ground.

"There it sleeps, waiting in silence. For a little while, it is as patient as the earth enduring until in due season it is awakened and called forth. The seed receives water, soil, and light into itself enabling it to transform. A tree is born. Through the four seasons it grows, each year is marked by a separate ring at its core that records its journey through time.

"You can touch the bark, smell and taste the fruit. You can sense the roots reaching down into the ground and the way the leaves reach up drinking in the fiery ecstasy of the sun. You can become the tree in your mind so there is nothing else in your awareness than what you gaze upon.

"If you see the world in this way without thoughts intervening, your mind replicates the vibration of the tree. If you were to speak to the tree it would reply to you mind to mind in a language that nature employs—of vitality, of life force, the sensations and perceptions of being alive, of existing within a specific environment, of being cloaked by both light and darkness, of expanding, of gaining strength, and of reproducing itself in a song of separation and reunion through which what has gone before appears now in a new form.

"In this way, you step outside of human time and perceive life in universal form. Similarly, if you gaze upon a rock, you sense millions of years gone by. You can enter its heart and understand silence enduring for ages, of being a part of a mountain as it lifts and towers above the land and as the mountain erodes and breaks down again.

"Herein is another form of wisdom—a clarity of perception that perceives the world in a way that nature understands. All things, no matter how long they may endure, are fragile. Everything that has form has a beginning and an end—the events of history are like images in a dream—they appear and then they are gone. In this practice the mind is refined so that its vibration can encompass years, ages, and eons as if they are but a moment of time.

"If you gaze upon a river or a stream, your mind takes on that vibration. Water adapts to each moment without clinging to any form it had in the past. And yet you can also comprehend the movement of the stream, its past and its future, from where it has come and to where it flows.

"Mist, clouds, and fog on a hillside form as rising warm air cools flowing over the hills at the end of a valley. Drops of rain fall on leaves, running down to the tip, dropping through the air, and sink into the ground. Or, in rivulets running down, they form a stream or splash in a mountain pool before flowing on.

"The stream turning and swirling around rocks is caught in the spell of gravity's pull until finally a lake or sea is found. There the stream joins with that watery expanse even as water in a falls lets go into the embrace of air and space as it falls.

"Gaze upon the stream and you experience pure innocence—it gives all of itself in every moment without holding anything back.

"And as for will, what is like unto magma rising up from deep in the earth to form a volcano thousands of feet high? Overflowing like an artery of the earth pulsing to the earth's heartbeat, it forms new land. Mountains explode. Great calderas burn. Cinder cones fill and spill as lava flows to the sea in streams of molten rock more viscous than water.

"Fire is hot, burning, devouring, seething, craving to expand and to be free overcoming all boundaries. If you gaze upon the volcano and allow your mind to join with its power, then you understand not just the will of a human being or even of a great warrior. You understand what it is to be joined from the core of your being to the powers unfolding the universe.

"How can a man ever understand or master himself unless the forces of nature—earth, air, fire, and water—flow freely through his soul? Unobstructed and with perfect clarity, he is beyond all fear or desire to attach to one form in this moment of time or identify with another form in that moment of time.

"To be free is to be in your consciousness like a mirror that can reflect perfectly anything that exists without blur or distortion. And to reflect perfectly is to be able to reproduce in your mind the exact energy and vibration of what you gaze upon.

"This is the mind that is able to join with another's mind so there is no separation. And in the joining there is something wonderful that happens—you know each other so well it is as if you have become brothers and sisters.

"And yet, in reflecting what the other is in your heart, you are able to speak to another with the voice at the core of his own being. You have become his guardian and the perfect companion who will walk beside him and assist him in fulfilling his deepest desires and dreams."

And then the Buddha pauses and gazes at the great warrior. And the Buddha speaks and says, "If you could see yourself through my eyes in this moment as I see you now you would attain perfect enlightenment."

And the warrior replies, "I see myself through your eyes. I see with your mirror like clarity and with your mind of boundless light. I feel what your soul feels—infinite peace. I respond as you respond with perfect empathy and unrestrained receptivity in which two become one so all separation is overcome."

And Buddha says, "You have become a second Buddha comprehending all that I am. Go now and accomplish what I myself have not done—defeat war itself and eliminate it forever from the earth."

Buddha was walking down the road one day and a woman was passing by on the other side. And she stops and comes over and says, "Why don't you ever speak about love? All you talk about is detachment and compassion. Becoming free of suffering is your obsession."

And Buddha responds, "Oh. You want to know about joining with another so that you feel one with your lover forever? The fact is I teach detachment and meditation because loving another consciously requires a very deep level of awareness—like a deep dreamless sleep in which you are nevertheless fully awake.

"Here time stops and the outer world ceases to exist. And here the awareness of your body and your heart and another's reach such a degree of bliss that only oneness exists.

"In this age of the world humanity is not yet ready to put aside ego and selfishness in order to experience this. But when the time is right many others like you shall demand as you are doing now that the mysteries of love be revealed in their full power and glory.

"Because you are inspired by the beauty of what it is to be alive I give you now this gift that shall remain with you forever—

"Your lover shall be as a stream. Sit beside him or meditate with him and he shall be with and inside of you dreaming your deepest dreams.

"Your lover shall be as the sea—love shall flow around and inside of you without barriers or boundaries.

"Your lover shall be as the highest mountains of the earth whose shoulders are caressed by the sky. Your oneness with your lover shall open your eyes. You shall see which nations shall fall and which nations shall rise. You shall see into the intricate designs of the human mind and what is within and behind all desires so that you are able to make others feel fully alive.

"Your lover shall be the thundering lightning of the storm. The two of you shall express the wild passion of the clouds that walk across the earth delivering nurturing rain to the flowers, trees, and fields.

"By becoming one with another to the degree you desire the human race shall put aside its ancient loneliness and shame, its greed and hatred. New dreams of love shall awaken in the human heart as the captain of a ship finds peace in returning to his home port."

One day Melchior (a priest magician also known as a Magi) came to visit Balthasar in ancient Persia. And Melchior said to Balthasar, "Tell me again about this practice you are doing."

Balthasar replies, "Emissaries from King Porus in India journeying to Rome left us texts written about a man they call Buddha. I have been studying them and have developed my own idea of how to practice his teachings."

Melchior goes on, "I only ask because I notice that you have changed. You are different. Instead of the old you—heavier than gold, serious as a bull elephant, and watchful as a lioness—your presence feels to me as light as air and flowing like water. What exactly is your mediation?"

Balthasar answers, "The Buddha figured out how to overcome all negative emotions—sorrow, sadness, depression, greed, anger, selfishness, pride, hated, malice, and so forth. One need only focus the mind so it becomes nothing. This is a nothing that is there before the earth and the sky were created, for if there is no self to grasp, to defend, or to grieve, then none of these emotions appear within one's consciousness."

Melchior, laughing, "Good for you. I assume you as nothing can still carry out all your priestly functions? I mean, kings still need to be crowned, disciples initiated, and wise counsel given to guide the nations. We would hate to have you retire to a cave in order to perfect your meditation."

Balthasar says, "The mediation in no way changes my activities. But it has an interesting effect on those around me."

Melchior continues pocking fun at Balthasar. Waving his hands in the air he says, "I am fading. I am fading. Take away my negativity along with the earth and the sky and nothing remains of me."

Balthasar says, "Actually, that might happen to some people. You see, though in the meditation the mind becomes nothing, this nothingness still has influence. It takes those who are high and haughty and makes them low. It takes the lowly and the humble and exalts them. It takes the path of life that is twisted and crooked and makes it straight as a Roman road. It takes those who are weary and exhausted and turns them into Greek athletes. And it takes the impure who are filled with filth inside and purifies them as with a refiner's fire."

Melchior asks, "And how does this nothingness accomplish this?"

Balthasar says, "Because there is no form or image in it, no substance, no light, no matter at all, and because it is a state of primordial awareness that exists before anything came into being, it automatically reveals the original nature of anything that comes near to it."

Melchior says, "Wait a moment. This sounds so familiar. Six hundred years ago, King Nebuchadnezzar captured many Jews and brought them to Babylon. We still have many of their sacred texts in our archives. I read one of them by a prophet Isaiah who spoke like you. He said, 'Every valley shall be exalted, and every mountain and hill shall be made low ....'"

"Isaiah also prophesized of a king of the Jews, a messiah, who is to be born in Judea. A most unusual king. He shall have no stately form nor splendor. He will be despised and rejected of men; a man acquainted with grief. What kind of king is this?"

"Don't you see the truth of it?" Asks Balthasar. "He who comes down from heaven cloaked in the light of the sun shall blind the eyes of those who look upon him. He will teach neither rituals nor doctrines, and he will anoint no priests. His religion is as simple as the air we breathe and the water we drink—we are to care for each other is the summation of all his teachings."

"I don't think the world is ready for him," says Melchior.

"Neither do I," says Balthasar. "But that will not keep him from trying."

"You know," says Melchior. "Something strange has happened to me. This is why I came to see you. You are more skilled in dream interpretation than I am. My spirit guide appeared to me in a dream and said, 'When a star appears, follow it and offer gifts to a child in a land to the West.'"

Balthasar replies, "Then tell the others to prepare for a journey. We must be ready when this star rises."

Sometimes when I meditate
He awakes inside of me
On occasion he speaks:

I studied Buddhism
To clear my mind
I studied the way of the sword
To better serve my lord
My inner silence was so complete
I could hear others words before they speak
I could perceive their future acts
When and where they would attack
The past and future are the same
There is nothing permanent that remains.

I reply,
I carry on your work
I am a knight of the Goddess of the earth
My inner silence is so complete
I hear angels when they speak
And the elements
Of water, earth, air, and fire
Reveal to me their mysteries.

Sometimes when I meditate
I awake within my future self
He says to me,
I carry on your work
There is an inner stillness so complete
It embraces the universe
The dreams you once dreamed

Have now become reality—
Justice fills the earth

Before the Phone, Radio, or TV

Before the phone, radio, or TV
Before internet, twitter, or electricity
There were the stars at night
Each filling the mind with its light
The eye perceives with different sight
The planets, the constellations,
The celebration of the seasons
Easy in them to see
The wonders fate decrees
Men of might rising to lead nations
Ominous portents of disastrous events
Yet underneath it all
A great harmony
The mystery of time
The unfolding of history
Here on display God's heart
A great stillness
Conceiving, nurturing, and embracing
All opposites and change
He who fails to find this stillness in himself
Is like a sailor at sea
Without destination, charts,
Without compass, or home port.

Cornelius was a priest of the Temple of Apollo in ancient Rome. This temple was built by Emperor Octavian in gratitude for his victory over Sextus Pompeius at the Battle of Naulochus in 36 BC and over Mark Anthony and Cleopatra at the Battle of Actium in 31 BC. The Temple was located at a site where a lightning bolt had struck the interior of Octavian's property on the Palatine. It was dedicated on October 9 of 28 BC.

Now the story is told of wise men who journeyed from the East to Israel to pay homage to a new born king. When a new world teacher is born someone usually sees it in a dream or vision. And sometimes there are seers, prophets, priests, mystics, and others who sense that something unusual is about to appear in history.

Cornelius was one of these. After all, three and a half centuries later Constantine defeated his enemies and became emperor in Rome due to a vision given to him by the god of the sun. Constantine then converted to Christianity because in his mind the link between Jesus and the sun could not be denied. Cornelius, similar to Constantine, recognized that Jesus reflected the light of the sun.

Decades after the Magi had offered their gifts, Cornelius journeys by sea to Palestine after the storms of winter had ceased. And once there Cornelius meets Jesus just as Jesus is about to teach on a hillside.

Cornelius walks up to Jesus and says, "I have come some distance to ask you a question. As a small token of my good will, I give to you this pearl which I have sold all that I possess in order to buy. If you are willing, tell me the truth of who you are. You speak in parables to the masses and they do not understand. But with me I ask you to speak plainly that I might be transformed by the light that is within you."

Accepting his gift, Jesus replies, "I am not the sun come down from heaven and cloaked in flesh that you might perceive God's presence on earth. Rather, gazing upon me, you see a mirror that reflects the light of the Creator. As a mirror is free of attachment, I am here to free mankind from greed, selfishness, hatred, and loneliness.

"You ask me about the truth in which I abide. My actions and teachings arise from a heart filled within infinite joy. I stand here now in front of you. But I am equally within you, around you, and within each person you meet. You only need open your eyes and your heart to see this and to feel it. Become as I am—the light of love that illuminates the heart in every man."

Cornelius returns to Rome and once again assumes his duties as a priest of the Temple of Apollo. But he was not the same man. It is as if he has been reborn.

A half hour later after speaking to Cornelius, Jesus goes up and sits on a hillside. And as is recorded in the Gospel of Matthew, Jesus speaks to the crowd gathered before him, "The kingdom of heaven is like a man who discovers a pearl of great value. And he goes and sells all that he has to purchase it."

B lessed are those who trust, for they have entered the kingdom of heaven.

Blessed are those who pass through their inner darkness without fear or shame, for they shall attain freedom.

Blessed are those who find the divine within themselves, for they shall fill the earth with justice as water covers the seas.

Blessed are those whose minds are as open and clear as the sky, for their peace shall be as a sea that has no shores and as a stream that flows from the dawn of time to the ends of eternity.

Blessed are those who transform conflict into harmony, malice into nobility, and war into peace, for these are the children of the creator and nothing shall be hidden from them.

Blessed are those who meet others in their darkest place and walk beside them back into the light, for there is no greater or more sacred celebration of life.

Blessed are those who let go and flow as each moment unfolds, for they shall see through the eyes of God.

Blessed are those who create love where love does not exist, for these have passed the final test and now embody in their souls the mystery of the universe.

There is linear time in which we exist. One day follows another in sequential order. And major events of significance we place in context and call it history.

On the other hand, there is akasha—a boundless, quantum reality containing all possibilities and all opportunities. It is an awareness that penetrates through space and time without attachment to a specific form, image, tradition, or lineage that restricts one's vision or imagination. Put another way, the past and future are here right now in this moment with equal presence and authority.

Akasha is flexible and creative. With it we can imagine that somewhere in space and time every need is met, every desire satisfied, every ideal fulfilled, every dream made real, every quest accomplished, happiness found, peace maintained, and love attained.

And so I contemplate my version of H.G. Wells' time machine. I imagine it as being physically here in front of me. I climb in. My time machine has a control panel with a dial that locates when and where a desire is satisfied or a dream made real.

I set the dial on "happiness found" and then I turn the machine on. The world around me whirls, a vortex swirls, and I am "Adrift on a sea of motionless time, where I come to see there are worlds enough for becoming myself," says Frank Waters in his book, Pumpkin Seed Point.

The engine hums. Time moves forward yet I myself am changing as time whirls around me. Oh I can produce happiness simply by concentrating. The chakras, the psychic aspect of our nervous system, come loaded with everything you might want. But chakras and concentration are not enough.

My time machine stops. Its program has produced a world for me where happiness is now a reality. I climb down and look around. A woman walks up. I look into her eyes. She is very real. She takes my hand and says to me, "I love you with all my heart."

Is it that simple? Another to walk at my side on the path of life? There is an inner desire for higher things—for justice, for truth, for wisdom, for a stillness that embraces the universe; and yet perhaps the most crucial thing—the inner self and the outer world joined as one through love.

I could stay longer. Perhaps write a novel about what I experience here or research the culture, discover how this world works. I linger for an hour and then I return to my time machine.

I set my dial back to 12/26/2015, 2:56 PM. The machine hums. The vortex swirls.

I return to the present from that future world with the scent of happiness surrounding me.

Son: "Dad?" Dad: "Yes son." Son: "I think this would be a good time for you to pass down to me your esoteric, oral tradition."

Dad: "What kind of tradition did you have in mind?"

Son: "I was thinking that since you are a 32nd degree Mason and since 14 U.S. presidents were Masons along with 13 signers of the Constitution maybe you have some sort of Masonic truth you could whisper into my ear so that I can make the transition from childhood to manhood?"

Dad: "Actually, all my Masonic initiations were more or less just social events. It was about making business connections. The Masons at this time in history have lost all their ties to the original magic that governed the unfolding of the universe."

Son: "Well then, in your travels in the Middle East, perhaps you met some Sufis who initiated you into the evocation of archangels which you can pass down to me so that I can speak to the archangels myself face to face. I would like to see for example the sky filled with vast choirs of heavenly hosts as it does when one sees Gabriel. Or else I would like to speak to Michael so that any battle I undertake in life results in absolute victory."

Dad: "Actually, all the Sufi masters I met told me more or less that there are no Sufis without orthodox Islam. Though the magic is there in no small measure, it would have been like trying to get Billy Graham to explain to you how to enter the presence of God. He never had any interest in God, just on setting the world on fire with his brand of evangelism."

Son: "Well, how about China? I mean you were the attorney for a number of major U.S. corporations when they set up their first factories in China. Did you perchance meet any Taoist masters who taught you how to gather and refine male Yang Jing, the masculine sexual essence, so that it transmutes into the Golden Flower producing a body of light and also astral immortality?"

"I mean I am on the verge of puberty. And I sure do not want to be a slave to my sexual desires the rest of my life, desires that can never truly be satisfied because they are in their essence insatiable and unending."

Dad: "Well, actually I spent a few months with each of two Taoist masters. But it turns out that their practices only work within the context of a feudal society in which men dominate women.

"Believe me. If I had any capacity whatsoever to be free of my insatiable and utterly unsatisfactory sexual desires you would never have been conceived."

Son: "Well, I know you lived in England for two years and were in cahoots with the aristocracy. Did any of them by chance make it part of their study to investigate the ancient traditions of the druids? I know for a fact that the poet, William Butler Yeats, was the chief of the Order of Bards, Ovates, and Druids, though no one in university literature departments knows that about his life."

Dad: (Waving his hand). "Yes. Yes. I was required to put on a robe and attend druid ceremonies in groves and among standing stones. But the druids, like Steiner's Waldorf schools, never reconciled the incomprehensible pace and acceleration of modern technology—you know, Ford, Edison, the Wright Brothers, Einstein, Heisenberg, Hubble, and Oppenheimer—with the exploration and integration of the soul. These two worlds, of the inner and outer self, have and still remain separate for thousands of years.

"Is that it? Or is there something else you have on your mind?"

Son: "Wait. What about theosophy and the West's gradual understanding of yoga—you know, Shakti ascending the spine and joining with Shiva in the crown chakra through the refinement and purification of the nadis and vitality in the physical body? Weren't you located in Mumbai for six months where you helped write the regulations governing the Bombay stock exchange?"

Dad: "It is true. You can't really walk from one end of town to the other without running into several Swamis or students of gurus who invite you to meet their masters.

"Yes. Yes. I caught the scent of bliss in which the gurus sit with their intoxicating chants and their bright smiles and auras of radiant light. The thing is my body cannot twist and bend to sit in a lotus position. And seeking God is not part of my family tradition in any way similar to what occurs every day and everywhere in India."

Son: "Well, I know when you first got out of college you worked for two years in Tuba City. While you were there didn't you ever attend a Navaho sand painting ceremony like the Blessing Way? You know, where the individual's body and soul are renewed by identifying with the gods of creation. They chant:

In Tsegihi [White House],
In the house made of the dawn,
In the house made of the evening light

"Or else you must have met some Navaho or Hopi shaman who possessed mysterious psychic powers?"

Dad: "No. I never made it to a sand painting ceremony. I was once invited by a drummer to a pow wow that lasted all night until dawn. I was the only white man there. Luckily, I had a few cartons of cigarettes in the trunk of my car. I gave them out freely. I was very popular.

"As for shaman, try reading Carlos Castaneda's writing on the Yaqui sorcerer Don Juan. His writing is very imaginative the way he romanticizes the desert. But in the end he died of liver failure and of too much sex. If you are trying to make it through puberty, Carlos Castaneda would be the wrong person to help you.

"No, the best that men have come up with in regard to taking command of their sexuality is found in the Amish, the Hasidic

Jews, the Orthodox Muslims with their four wives, the orthodox Hindus, or the polygamists of Utah, etc. They have clearly defined gender roles and so the male is able to survive intact in those circumstances. But now everyone takes for granted that clear gender definitions have come to an end with the beginning of modern society."

Son: "Okay. I am onto you. I see what you are up to here. You actually do have something worth saying to me, don't you? You just wanted me to set up a dramatic context so that what you say is appreciated for what it is."

Dad: (sighing and taking a deep breath, exhaling). "This is what they do not teach you in sex education in school or in the soft porn of Hollywood movies—

"A woman's form is a magic mirror. Her body is shaped in a way that a man's mind can neither grasp nor imagine. She distills and embodies the beauty of nature. Men have no such reflective power.

"A woman can pour a man a cup of love. She can offer a man to drink of her body and soul In so doing, she gives him a taste and a vision of what is hidden in himself.

"But a woman cannot complete for a man the journey he must take in order to find that beauty and oneness with nature within himself. His union with her will always be incomplete if he cannot first unite with the feminine spirit.

"Value truth as much as love. Persevere with all your strength when you gaze into this mirror that is femininity. See beyond your personal desires.

"The path to self-knowledge is full of obstacles and barriers. There are places within the soul where men may not go. The waters are too deep. The flow is too pure. If a man dares enter the feminine mysteries he will drown.

"And there are places within the spirit where women may not enter: beyond the worlds of form opposites are overcome and the joy found there is infinite. If a woman dares enter these masculine mysteries she will be burnt to a crisp.

"Now here is the epiphany, the risk, the reason why a man ejects 500 million sperm with the possibility of only one fertilizing the female's egg. This drama is played out on a microscopic level in every human birth that takes place on earth—

"If a man could so enter and survive the Earth's womb, to dissolve within that dark place and not lose his masculinity; if a woman could journey into the heart of the sun and survive its fires and its light without loss of her femininity, then their spirits would no longer be subject to the gender limitations imposed by their anatomy and by society—

"They will have cast off their mortality and put on immortality. Such individuals are then appointed as the guides and Guardians of the Earth and of evolution."

Son: "You would pass down to me a spirit quest for something that is impossible to attain?"

The father holds his hand out palm down and shakes it left and right. Then he says, "Well. Let me put it this way. I wish you luck and success where I myself failed."

Son: "Is that it, then?"

Dad: "A Zen master once told me when I worked in Japan, as we were sipping sake while sitting late at night on the steps of an old Shinto shrine, 'The perfect path is always easy to follow. Strive hard to find it!'"

Son: "I do not feel I am getting your full attention."

The father looks at his son for a minute and then he says, "Okay. I was planning to set aside some money for your inheritance. But considering your relentless interest in initiation, I have a proposal.

"What if I put three million dollars into a foundation. When you are twenty-one years of age, you can take charge of this foundation. Call it a research institute dedicated to the rebirth of the Freemasons, but now it will be in another form without ties to any specific tradition.

"Rather, study all these traditions you have mentioned. Invite the various masters and gurus from all over the earth to come and give seminars. Extract the universal elements from each lineage and then use them to build a new system of spiritual training, one free of cultural bias. Distill a wisdom that is in harmony with the greater universe, for originally that was the ultimate aim of the Freemasons.

"Then develop a curriculum that anyone can study who wishes to play both a productive and a creative role in society.

"As I once discovered, perhaps you too will realize that it is up to you to become the man you wished your father had been. I can give you a means to start a journey. But it is your task, as it is each man's task, to become the person you wish to be."

Son: "Thank you. I will finish what you have begun."

Note: The astral plane that sustains the soul of every living being on earth appears in the form of a woman.

Astral Plane: "Tell me about your obsession."

Man: "The doctors have said my case is hopeless. They have never seen anything like it. They label it a terminal illness, a morbid obsession, or something worse."

Astral Plane: "And why do you suppose that is?"

Man: "Because I realize that women cannot give me what I want."

Astral Plane: "Have you considered that you cannot give women what they want?"

Man: "Women are easy. They want security, social status, happiness, love, intimacy, someone there for them who cherishes them, listens to them, and feels what they feel. They want a chance to be themselves and yet also know they are meeting another person's needs as well.

"A woman wants a man who at the beginning creates special moments for her and no other and who goes on creating special moments through all the years they share.

"Women feel more inside but need more external support to sustain those feelings and a strong social network is where they thrive. Men are more empty inside but need less external support other than sex to accomplish their purposes in life."

Astral Plane: "So tell me. What is it that you want from women?"

Man: "I want the physical intimacy without having to compromise or dumb down my masculinity to get it.

"Like any lover, I want her to feel what I feel. But I want so much more. I want her to be nurturing and caring and also to make me feel fully alive. I want her to make a serious effort to satisfy my deepest desires and also to enter my dreams and dream them with me.

"I want her to anoint me with a love that unites me to the deepest purposes of life. When I enter her, I want to feel that I am made new and joined to a universe of love.

"Most of all, I want her to inspire me; to see what I can be and then ask me to become that man who I have never met but who she already knows intimately."

Astral Plane: "I know you can say it better than that. Go ahead. Let it all out."

Man: "When I am fire, I want a woman who burns with me. When I am water, I want a woman who with pure innocence lets go into the flow, who is so much in the moment that past and future do not weigh upon her.

"When I am air, I want a woman who can be as free and as cold as the jet stream, as warm as the trade winds, and as gentle as a summer breeze.

"When I am earth, I want a woman who can become silence itself, more enduring than mountains, and more focused and abiding than a stone a billion years old.

"When I am the empty night sky I want a woman who can fill that void with the serenity of moon and the songs the stars sing.

"When I look into the past I want a woman who is there beside me, reliving the past with me. When I look into the future, I want a woman who sees what we can bring into being through the power of our two hearts joined.

"You think this is too much to ask?"

Astral Plane: "Is there a woman in all the earth who can meet your demands?"

"It sounds to me, that unlike any other man I have ever met, you have the ghosts of Christmas past, present, and future walking beside you. Do you know that story of Charles Dickens, A Christmas Carol?"

Man: "Yes."

Astral Plane: "The three ghosts lead Scrooge to realize and to say exactly what they wanted to teach him without actually telling him what it was.

"He says after seeing his future burial place in a grave yard,

"'Why show me this, if I am past all hope? Assure me that I yet may change these shadows you have shown me, by an altered life! The Spirits of all Three (past, present, and future) shall strive within me. I will not shut out the lessons that they teach. Oh, tell me I may sponge away the writing on this stone!'"

Man: "When you put it that way and when I hear myself talking about what I want from a woman, I see now what has been missing from my account. I do not want a woman to do all these things for me. That would be selfish, vain, and lacking in imagination. I want to be the person who can do all these for others."

Astral Plane: "You know, Buddha became a symbol of what the mind is when it embodies absolute freedom and perfect clarity.

"You too have a quest. It is to embody the astral plane, but not to create a new religion with fanatical and insanely insecure followers attached to manmade beliefs. Your task is to open men's eyes so they are filled with visions and open their hearts so they can dream a new world into being.

"Do you know what non-linear time is?"

Man: "I have a basic notion."

Astral Plane: "The past, present, and future are equally real and fully present in this moment now. For those who understand this, all things are possible. If you feel this in your heart, your love is inexhaustible.

"I anoint you with this love. Share it with others and transform the world."

The Winds

"One day a woman will love me as the wind loves the sky. When it is warm, she sails high. When it is cold, she clings to me so I am never alone."

Jack Allen: I am a farmer and our lives are hard. For those who ply my trade, having a wife who is loyal and enthusiastic is rare indeed. Having a woman in your life who loves you with all of her heart is more than rare. It is next to impossible.

And yet, I dreamed I met a woman who loved me with all of her heart. She brought my life into focus; looking back, I feel I was not really alive until we met; it is like we had always known each other, like we were meant to meet and share our lives together.

I know. That is a lot of feeling packed into one dream. But she came to me again and again in my dreams. It became a regular event. Some might say that when I sleep I am living a parallel incarnation. Or maybe she is just an old fashioned "dream lover." Repeat visits are part of the package. Or maybe these dreams have come to challenge my assumptions about what might have been or still could be.

Now loving me with all of her heart does not mean she is not critical or fails to give me accurate feedback. It does not mean I can take her for granted. And it does not mean I can take more than I give. But it does mean when she deems it appropriate she follows my lead.

And she loves children—a woman who loves children these days seems to be a contradiction. Where is her ego, her desire for self-realization, or her career? She would have to be aware of non-linear time—that past and future are already in this moment joined.

In my dreams, I built an addition to the house, a room above the roof that looks out in all directions on the farm. Soft curtains and open, screened windows that cool the room with a breeze. I added a large skylight so we can see the stars and constellations at night as we lie side by side.

These dreams are so real when I am having them I cannot tell if I am awake or asleep. I wake up in the morning and go to find the stairs leading up to addition, but it is not there. Yet I catch her scent. In the dream, we have already had breakfast. Eating breakfast again almost seems redundant.

Sometimes in the dreams we make love so slowly that time seems to stop. It may begin with touch and sometimes only with breath before we kiss or caress. I am aware of the air going in and out of my chest and I am aware of the oxygen in the air—a planet like earth that has oxygen in the atmosphere to this extent only exists where life has been at work producing it.

The air is a sea possessing currents and tides, jet stream and trade winds, the thunderstorm with wind shear and lightning thundering. In my mind, I become this sea and as this sea I surround her and I am within her, nurturing and protecting her. In the awareness of air our two souls join.

And in the joining we are weightless, free, flowing continuously and harmoniously balancing opposites—hot and cold, wet and dry, low and high, magnetic and electric, calm or turbulent, gentle breeze and violent gusts.

Our breathing slows. The sky is in our chest, the winds our breath.

I feel the oxygen coursing through my bloodstream and I feel the oxygen moving through her as it moves through me. We become one body.

The wind caresses the leaves of the trees. It carries the seeds. It brings the rain. The wind inhales and water evaporates in the thrill of freedom rising, vapors and moisture with clouds forming.

The wind exhales and trees breathe in carbon dioxide. Our lungs and the trees share the same breath.

The wind exhales and the barometer drops, rain falls. Storm clouds fly with winds that wail, torrential rain flailing. Tornadoes and storm cells spinning, water renewing the earth.

This is our foreplay as we sit and watch each other during the day—I notice her chest rising, falling. I am the air flowing through her chest and she is the breath that touches my lips, that jostles my hair, that kisses my neck.

She follows my lead and I lead her to a stillness that embraces the four seasons, day and night, earth and the heights, youth and old age moving with laughter and delight.

The Sea

"One day a woman will love me as the ocean loves the shore. All night long I listen to the waves breaking like the sound of her heartbeat as she lies next to me."

Late at night, the full moon reaches its height. I am spooning with her, holding her from behind, skin to skin.

I am certain there are women on earth that when you touch them, your hand resting gently on her arm, there is no longer two of you. Rather, she, you, and the sea become one being without separation, having cast off individual identities.

Spooning with this woman, I feel the love. It is as water, fluid and flowing. She and I are now the open expanse of waves stretching from horizon to horizon, the waters that stir and circle between continents.

This sea vibrates with feelings and sensations that are soothing, releasing, renewing, purifying, tender, soft, caressing, with happiness welling up and overflowing.

My fingertips, my palms drift upon her shoulder sliding down her arm, reaching out and resting on her belly—I sail as a bird upon the wind searching across the oceans of her soul for new islands to call my home.

My hand continues on, gently caressing the curve of her hips —I find myself in a dark forest at night following the sound of one bird singing, singing to me of a dream I let fly away from me, escaping from my life to be free; but now it has returned, charmed by her beauty and by this touch upon her hips in this night of quiet ecstasy.

Our chests rise and fall together in motion driven by the same tide. The moon sets sail to solar winds illuminating her naked skin. I no longer know who I am except a path of love that has no end.

Our hips join as the stream winds through the crevice of the valley, mirth and laughter splashing down, as the sea enfolds the mountains in her depths, the whale's song echoing through the hills.

Geese fly across the moon. The leaves of birch trees shiver. A solitary bird sings. Cats' paws ripple upon the surface of a lake. Gusts of wind pulsate.

Her love shapes my life as the hands of a sculptor mold the clay. Closing my eyes, I hear a harpist play the notes of the song within her heart.

I fall asleep at peace. And when I awake she is still here with me. The feeling of a woman is like a pool flowing beneath a mountain. No sun dawns. No moon rises. Yet the water is luminous, cool, soft, soothing amid transparent light, silence dancing, the taste of love a secret sharing heart to heart.

She whispers gently, softly as her body presses back against mine—"You are my soul."

There have been men such as Sir Francis Drake and Magellan who sailed forth, their ships encircling the earth. Courageous and bold, firm were their hands upon the helm. With sextant and charts they mastered the dark. But in their eyes the blue green sea did not dream. Sir Francis Drake and Magellan did not know love such as this—

The expanse of love within these depths—a billion years and she brings life into being; and at night for this length of time she has been absorbing the light of the stars in the sky. Listening to them, she distills their stories and their songs into one taste, one bliss in which she feels one with the universe.

"And the sea shall grant each man new hope as sleep brings dreams of home." More than Columbus knew, the embracing sea dreams the fulfillment of each man's dreams. Innocence—the past does not shape her endless giving in the present. Wonder—the unknown universe coming through and revealing itself in each moment forever new.

She turns and faces me. I love her eyes, so quiet and peaceful, a place to let go and forget who I am. I catch the scent of the sea. I hear the waves breaking. I see through her eyes the man I am meant to be. She dreams him into being.

The Earth

"One day a woman will love me as chemistry binds molecules forming new kinds of matter. At her touch, the most primordial instincts hidden in nature become transparent, luminous light creating paths of wonder as our bodies join together."

Lying together, her butt pressed against my body, our legs touching, our feet rubbing.

When I was young, I once sat back to back against a girl. My back heated up so it became quite hot, my shirt drenched in sweat. She told me later she was having orgasms on and on. But I was too naïve at the time to notice such things.

I once sat next to a girl, our backs leaning against Bell Rock. It was like the hill wrapped its arms around me. And the mesas before us and in the distance woke up and spoke. They said, "We stand ready to serve."

In my early twenties, I often went out in the desert or into valleys. I sat amid mountains. In that silence with no one within miles, I listened patiently. I waited.

The weight of the earth, its gravity and silence, reached out and wrapped its arms around me, cradling me. Each woman has her own nervous system, her own sensuality, and her own relationship to her body. When you touch some women, you can feel her skin and nervous system reaching out and touching you back with the same sensitivity.

For me, trees are mostly feminine. When I touch them, they wake up. They come alive. They feel what I feel inside. They share with me their dreams and their visions.

Flowers are not just flowers. They have voices. They are the earth singing.

When I sit in the desert, in valleys, or among mountains, time grows old. Billions of years sit and wait patiently with me. And yet in each moment a new world around me unfolds.

In the hills about me, the mountain lion, the bobcat, the lynx, the bear, the deer, the elk, the javelina, the coyote, the badger, the racoon, the squirrel, the chipmunk, the rabbit, the great horned owl, the hawk, the eagle—they are all there. I am aware of them as they are aware of me. I see through their eyes.

In their bodies, they are so much more alert and alive than I am in my body. Their senses are sharper. Their instincts carefully designed to survive in their habitats.

Something is happening as I wait in the silence, the circle of the earth moving silently amid the heavens. Can a woman reach out and touch a man, knowing his body so well it is as if they have become one being?

The earth reaches out to touch me through the body of the woman lying next to me. If there is an angel from legend or theology, a celestial horticulturist who tends the plants, flowers, and trees in that mythical Garden of Eden, then she too is here touching me. Her skill is the art of enhancing vitality so as to develop perfect health. She will never be satisfied until we attain immortality. Such gifts do not come cheap.

That ancient garden, that oasis hidden in some vast desert, is guarded by the formidable power of silence. This silence is an unknown terrain and an invisible mountain range. No army can climb it. No commander or general can penetrate it and no reconnaissance plane can fly over it.

You can neither lay siege to it nor assault it. This silence is the will of the universe moving unobstructed toward its goal.

More than light or darkness, silence defines sight; more than thought and words, silence defines understanding; more than movement or volition, silence defines action. If you learn to sit and wait in silence, you can formulate plans of action that no one else can imagine.

There are women cloaked in silence. It is a feeling you get sitting next to them. Oh, they do all the normal things normal people do. But if you touch them, hold their hands, or lie next to them, like an invisible whirlwind descending, a power takes hold of you. The mind no longer uses thoughts to think. Decades, hundreds, or thousands of years seem like a watch in the night.

Then historical events seem like they have just happened. Washington escaping from Long Island, winter defeating Napoleon at Moscow, Pope Leo speaking with Attila the Hun—it is like watching the 6 o'clock news.

At the touch of her body against mine, the distant past and the distant future draw near. This is what is happening—I put aside my distractions and my fears, my insecurities, my anxieties, and any need for external validation. I focus only on the deepest things I care about in the depths of my soul. She reveals the work I can love with all of my heart.

My life has been lived in solitude. And yet even here she draws near, cuddling me, as intimate as the earth, as breath, as heartbeat, as this body I wear. At her touch, silence blossoms like a flower, its scent revealing the inner light shining in all things.

Silence whispers to me, "You have learned my secrets. You hear the song the earth sings to other planets. You have followed ancient paths men have long forgotten. The barriers dissolve separating life and death, this world and the next, the kingdoms hidden at the edge of the five senses, the realms of the soul where saints and seers are afraid to go.

"That separation, that cold, cruel loneliness that haunts the human heart down through all ages, my greatest secret you already know—there really is no separation, but each person must learn this on his own."

I dreamed I met a woman who loved me with all of her heart. All the mysteries of nature reveal themselves in the presence of her love.

The Fire

"One day a woman will love me as the moon loves the sun— in her dreams, she dances with me until we are one."

I sense the difference between my body temperature of 98.6 degrees and the temperature of the air around me of 73 degrees. I sense the micro movements of air, tiny updrafts from my skin and the faint moisture evaporating. My body shines bright with infrared light.

Relaxing, I focus on my body temperature. My parasympathetic nervous system kicks in as my brain waves change from beta to alpha releasing dopamine, endorphins, oxytocin, and opiates into my bloodstream. My metabolism burning furiously races to maintain equilibrium.

Even when she enters the same room, there is the crackle, snapping, hissing, and buzzing of St. Elmos fire drifting across my skin. Ball lighting emerges from thin air. Subliminal lightning crashes and thunders. An entire storm rages with electrical particles, negative and positive charges, flashing, expanding, exploding, and colliding across the gap between us arching.

Do people not notice these things?

With her in the same room, my sympathetic nervous system awakes. My body temperature rises. My heart rate and blood pressure increase. My eyes dilate.

My lower brain with its primitive, instinctual drives and my frontal lobe with its imagination and foresight begin negotiations, bartering and trading to produce mutually satisfying solutions.

Again, I notice the difference in temperature between my body of 98.6 degrees compared to the temperature of the air around me of 73 degrees. I notice the difference in temperature between a cinder cone of 1,200 degrees and the temperature of the air around it of 73 degrees.

For the contemplative mind, there is little difference. Fire in the body and fire in nature share the same heart. They have the same burning hunger, the raging, craving, exploding desire to be set free, to be released so as to taste life, to be fully alive, and to find peace.

The pulse of blood within my body is the same pulsing and throbbing of the earth's artery. I share the earth's body, magma rising from the depths. The DNA molecule demands that consciousness become a master adept who can overcome all the obstacles life places before it.

The cumulonimbus clouds flowing over the earth with its squall line and supercells, wind shear and updrafts with warm air ascending, cooling, condensing, twelve miles high, downdrafts pulling the cool air down, drops forming, and precipitation.

In the space between her body and mine, like the space between the thunderstorm and the earth, I feel the same electrical particles charging, building, intensifying, raging with whirling, liquid fire, a frenzied, seething desire reaching the height of passion until lightning, as hot as the sun, arcs annihilating separation.

I am a thunderstorm. And though I wear a human body that needs rest and sleep, the lighting in me never stops. The charge is always building, intensifying, and exploding.

With another kind of passion, with innocence and wild purity, the moon's serenity fills the night, soothing and releasing. Whereas desire has a beginning and an end, she loses nothing by capturing the sun's nuclear fire as sunlight blazing in ice.

Without the emptiness of space, there can be no stars. With the nurturing environment of planets, there can be no life.

In her arms, fire, enchanted by her beauty, finds rest and peace. Two become one circle of life.

I dreamed I met a woman who loved me with all of her heart. For such a woman, complete mastery over fire is part of her art.

The Void

"One day a woman will love me with a stillness that embraces the universe. When I look into her eyes, I see all the stars in the night sky. When she touches my hand, I become space itself—I am within and a part of everything."

Farmer Jack Allen: I dreamed a woman came to me. Her aura was as black as the empty space that all the stars' embrace.

Prajnaparamita—the mother of all enlightened beings—her essence is emptiness. But she rarely if ever appears in anyone's dreams.

Yet the dream woman says to me, "Every ending, farewell, and good-bye is a sacred rite in my eyes." She is like the chief Judge of Saturn who, though detached and severe, is more passionate than any virgin, more intimate than heartbeat or breath.

"Every soul desires to transform the world through love." If the Ghost of Christmas Future is a woman, she reminds us of the consequences of failing to accomplish this.

This woman is a second conscience, a backup kicking in when we stop listening to the still, quiet voice speaking inside.

Too formidable and ominous to be a spirit guide. Too cosmic to be a spiritual consort. No twin flame burns this hot. No soul mate can create love from nothingness through her art.

King Indrabhuti asked Buddha, "Can you help me with my emotions?" And Buddha replied, "Oh. You want tantra. Take the vastness of the sky, the emptiness of the void, and clarity of the enlightened mind and fashion them into the form of a woman. She is flesh and blood. Her heart beats beneath her skin. She speaks. Look into her eyes."

This woman takes my right hand enfolding it between her palms. With my left hand I hold her hand from below. What do I feel?

Ah. This is a stillness that embraces the universe. Just what you would expect when the compassion and kindness arise from this depth.

Birth, old age, and the repetition of incarnations—years, ages, and eons between.

A father says to his son, "Finish your homework. Find a career. Work hard. Do your best. And when you have time at the end of the day or on weekends be aware that love is everywhere. It is in the wind, the sea, the fire of lightning, and the mountains and the trees."

Can you be too serious or sober when you make choices that shape your future? And yet life is like a lucid dream. If we wake up within it and, with enough imagination and concentration, we can change anything.

This woman whose essence is emptiness sits on my lap. What is her secret? It is innocence, trust, play, and happiness spontaneously embracing laughter and delight in all seasons of life and in all ages of time.

Sometimes to learn you have to have firsthand experience with a woman in the flesh. And sometimes to learn you have to first imagine it. Tantra is flexible as are dreams. In either you are free to consider any and all options.

PART III

ATLANTIS

An Ancient Order of Women, Part I: The Mirror

There was an ancient order of women
Whose magical beauty was so great
They could dissolve all malice and hate.
Every being was their friend.
The broken heart they could mend
And the lost soul was found again.
For 5,000 years they ruled in complete secrecy
Being free of the desire for fame and all vanity
Until in the end
Men sought knowledge instead of harmony
And power instead of beauty.

At the time, Sa was not yet a member of the High Council of Atlantis. She was still working through her studies at the Academy of Magic. Though none of the students or teachers at the Academy knew it, Sa was already an active member of a secret Order of women who had been influencing Atlantis from behind the scenes for thousands of years.

In that Order, each female initiate was assigned two to ten of the most powerful leaders in Atlantis to inspire and to guide. Sa's first assignment was a rogue mage named Alturo. A member of the High Council for many years, Alturo had resigned from the Council concerned about dangers to Atlantis that the High Council was not addressing.

Alturo went off to live by himself in a stone tower in the wilderness far from any of the cities of Atlantis. There he researched magic and studied the future. And these things he could do because he was one of the best magician scientists in Atlantis.

Sa herself picked Alturo to work on. She did not do this as a conscious decision with reasons and clear purposes. Instead, she could feel that Alturo was a nexus point through which great power flowed.

And this is what she did. Skilled in joining her mind to others within a state of lucid dreaming, she presented to Alturo while he slept an image of a magic mirror. Almost immediately Alturo realized he was in a lucid dream. But, as lucid dreams go, to Alturo this dream was as real as any reality.

Alturo actually was not worried about whether he was dreaming or awake. Being a mage who works with ritual tools, this magic mirror was utterly fascinating. Confronted with a phenomenon that defied explanation, he realized he had a perfect opportunity to learn something new about the universe.

Right away Alturo noticed four vibrations that defined how the mirror operates. First, like an actual mirror, the mirror had the vibration of extreme detachment. A mirror reflects what is in front of it while remaining unaffected.

But, in this case, the image existed in a three-dimensional space while the surface of the mirror remained two dimensional. This mirror was a symbol of empty space—the space itself in which all physical things appear.

If you look at something you have perspective and point of view. There is you and then there is the object. But what if you imagine your consciousness is space itself? Then anything you think about or focus on is within your consciousness. You are around it, inside of it, and the condition upon which its existence depends. The same detachment is there. It is just more encompassing.

Men, as well as all beings and spirits that are masculine, build a charge, assert their power, and release their energy to affect the world or some sphere of action. But this mirror, though detached, is utterly receptive. It has no point of view and no will to assert. And yet, as a mirror reflects every photon of light that touches it, this consciousness reflects every fiber of every nerve cell and brain wave within a person its focuses on. And like space itself, this receptive, reflective consciousness is not affected by what it reflects.

In another age of the world, Alturo would have simply said to himself, "Ah. Prajnaparamia, the mother of all enlightened beings —emptiness, consciousness without form or image." But it would be more than ten thousand years before Buddha would appear on earth to teach such things.

Alturo paused at this point. Mind as understood by Atlantean scientists and magicians was extremely clairvoyant in respect to matter. They sent their minds directly into metals, compounds, alloys, and crystals and developed technologies through direct mind-matter interactions.

But Atlantean scientists did not know about the nature of mind itself—that it is boundless light, an open space with multiple dimensions within it which do not rely on thoughts to think, to investigate, or to evaluate. This level of detachment embodied in this mirror did not exist in Atlantis. Alturo decided that when he had time he would investigate this state of mind to see what its uses and applications are.

The second thing Alturo noticed about the mirror was that it had perfect empathy and this empathy existed on different levels. To use the mirror you had to be totally detached as if you were empty space; and you had to be the other person in your mind, sensing the other's physical sensations as if you were wearing that person's body. You were then able to feel what that individual felt as if his feelings were your own. And you were able to think the other's thoughts with the same brain waves as that individual. The other's history and memories became yours as well.

Alturo grasped this right away because he understood that the body, soul, and mind each have their own karma. Someone can be loving and generous and yet all the same be narrow-minded and prejudiced. Someone can be brilliant in mind and wise and yet be emotionally insecure and vulnerable. Someone can be very strong physically and yet be easily frightened. Humans are a mixture and rarely if ever integrated much less conscious of their own weaknesses and folly.

But there was more. The mirror sitting in front of Aluro was not passive. It emitted several vibrations. One was like the sea surrounding the earth.

It was exactly as if Alturo had meditated on all the oceans of the earth until he sensed all that water and then felt that water was in and around himself. And yet having done so, that watery vibration localized itself as if it was flowing through the person reflected in the mirror.

In fact, Alturo felt this watery, flowing energy moving through himself as he sat in front of the mirror. And this watery energy was releasing, soothing, calming, and tranquilizing. It purified and healed.

Alturo could not recall having ever met a woman who passed onto him through her love and presence this release and happiness he was now experiencing. Alturo thought to himself, "It is a magic mirror and this is its magic. It does what it does."

Alturo next said to himself, "That healing love is taking place in linear time but its beauty goes deeper. The healing love is also non-linear. It is taking past, present, and future and uniting them into one, vast, all-inclusive moment. Time is a sea and even this life is but a small part of who I am and what I am to become."

Alturo felt a peace and well-being that the civilization of Atlantis knew little about. Because if they had known this peace they would not have engaged in experiments involving increasing levels of risk that threaten their own existence. And this they did because they felt numb inside and because the development of their minds had raced far ahead of the love within their hearts.

And so here we have Alturo in a lucid dream gazing at a mirror. And at this point he feels he has become the mirror and he is gazing back at himself. Except now he has the detachment of empty space combined with the love of the realm of mermaids who dwell in the energy underling the sea. And stepping outside of the stream of time, there is a timelessness that somehow mysteriously guarantees that all dreams will be fulfilled, all ideals made real, and all missions accomplished.

Now the thing about the feminine mysteries is that the fetus in the womb does not know where it is and does not need to know in order to be protected, nourished, and offered a perfect environment in which to grow. The ancient Order of women knew how to hide themselves from those they were influencing. They had no desire for fame and no need for glory to celebrate their gender's accomplishments. Receptivity itself is omnipotent power, a power our history has never imagined.

Alturo did not ask himself where this image of a mirror was coming from. And if he had tried to ask that question it would have vanished from his mind. The thing is that love, unlike will, can be one with others, protecting, inspiring, and guiding without individuals being aware of the source of their blessing and why a path of light has appeared before them.

Alturo noticed one other thing about the mirror. With the mirror present, he felt a part of a greater magnetic field that encompasses the planet—both the watery energy of the seas, the love and innocence of the mermaid realm, and the magnetosphere that protects the earth from the charged particles emitted by the sun.

It is this magnetic field that flows through and is within every living being on earth. And it is from this perspective of all-embracing love that the individual's unique path in life is most clearly seen. For all the varied forms of life that have and will appear on earth are sustained by it and live within it. If you feel this, then you feel a part of nature and, like the magnetic field itself, you exist to nurture, to protect, and to perfect.

As Alturo sat there looking at himself reflected in the mirror, he began laughing. And this was odd because Alturo was always deadly serious. He knew there was great danger facing Atlantis and he wanted to do something about it. But he was feeling joy, a joy that comes from feeling the universe reflected inside yourself.

Now I can review all these things the mirror was doing to Alturo—creating the harmony he felt inside himself, the healing love, the detachment, the power of beauty that unites all ages of the individual's life and also all life on earth into one experience.

But it is at this moment that Alturo realized what had been missing from his life. He did not have a student to pass his magical heritage down to. And the mirror was showing who that student was and where he could be found.

And so it was that Alturo took He'ad'ra as his disciple, an orphan without a royal or aristocratic bloodline. Alturo adopted him and raised him as his own child. And the mirror was not mistaken.

When He'ad'ra sought to enter the Academy of Magic, he lacked the noble bloodline required of applicants. But a member of the High Council, Heburus, out of respect for Alturo, offered He'ad'ra his own colors to wear. You could say He'ad'ra was adopted twice, once by Alturo, now deceased, and a second time by Heburus. Not long after that, He'ad'ra became the high priest of Atlantis.

Yet we could also say that He'ad'ra was adapted by a third person, namely Sa. Sa's love also shaped him and Atlantis through him.

There was an ancient Order of women. Behind the scenes and hidden, they discovered that the power of the feminine spirit is infinite.

AN ANCIENT ORDER OF WOMEN, PART II:
MOTHER AND DAUGHTER

Daughter: "Mother. I have noticed that there is an emptiness inside of men."

Mother: "True. Go on."

Daughter: "And even among men who are wise or who are initiates of the Mysteries, there remains a void inside them. Its offshoots are loneliness and an ancient sorrow that haunts them."

Mother: "Yes. Your observations are accurate. This is the case."

Daughter: "The question is then does our magic exist to fill this void so that separation is destroyed and replaced with intimacy, love, and beauty? Do we have this power? Or is there something men have to do for themselves that is quite beyond what we can comprehend?"

Mother: "At the very center of the feminine mysteries is the uterus—in each cycle of the moon, we become 100% open, empty, and receptive to accept the essence of the man into ourselves; to take what he is and to unite with it, nurturing and protecting, until new life is brought forth into the world.

"And this we can do not just with the seed of his body, but with his soul, mind, and spirit as well. We can so love and embrace the soul of any man so as to saturate him with love—every cell of his being—enfolded with bliss and ecstasy so that he lets go of the man he knows himself to be in order to become another man, one who transforms the world.

"We have the power to overcome all obstacles, karma, and past attachments that have shaped his identity and self-awareness. Such is the love we possess—to guard and to protect Atlantis from the darkness that assails it from all sides."

Daughter: "But there is a difference. I recall being in your womb. I recall being born. I recall the first years of my life. I am the same person now as I was as a child, though now I am more knowledgeable about the world. I have never been separate from your love. I have always sensed your protective aura around me, sustaining, healing, renewing, and inspiring me.

"But when I meditate on the souls of men it is not at all like that. If I turn within, I find you. And I find behind you a love that embraces the earth as the seas surrounds the lands. And further still, I find in myself a stillness that embraces the universe, all that exists and all that shall come to be. Whatever the events of the outer world, my inner world is whole and complete.

"But men do not experience this connection to the feminine. It is like nature cuts them off, forcing them to go on without this love. It is as if they are in search of an unknown land where they can make a new home."

Mother: "Their anatomy and testosterone propels them forward into the outer world. They must eke out a niche for themselves, establish and defend boundaries, compete to fashion a social identity and maintain a support group. A man by definition must take command of himself, of others, and of nature. They struggle to survive in a world where food, shelter, recognition, and even affection and love are in scarce supply.

"Amid this struggle, the knowledge and wisdom they acquire pertains not to love and union, but to survival and power. Understanding the way the world works is a matter of focusing on who is in charge, who has the strongest will, and who decides on the allocation of resources.

"Men will always define knowing themselves in terms of having the power to survive, to endure, and to flourish in the world as they find it."

Daughter: "Are you saying that the wisest of men are incapable of feeling a oneness with the universe from inside of them?"

Mother: "What do you feel when you use the word oneness?"

Daughter: "I feel my uterus—the cells, the tissue, the blood flow, and the muscles surrounding it, an inviting fertility longing and ready to accept, nurture, and to give birth. In my body, masculine and feminine unite to bring new life into the world.

"And underneath and behind my uterus is an open, empty, utterly receptive awareness embracing all of space and time. This oneness I sense is both in my body and in the greater universe. There is a continuum of love between me, life, society, and the world and this continuity is impossible to miss."

Mother: "Just how good are you? Place your consciousness in a member of the High Council."

Daughter: "I can do that. I can sense Tehuti the Second. I can tell you what he had for breakfast by sensing his stomach. I feel the tension in his lower neck. I can see through his eyes the room he is now in and the thoughts he thinks as he concentrates. I can feel his soul, his passions, his deepest desires, and the spiritual realizations that have guided him and made him who he is. I can release that tension in his neck and also feel so much a part of him that he no longer feels lonely or separate from nature.

"And beyond all of this I can enter the dreams he dreams at night and the dreams he has for his life and dream them along with him. But this any woman on earth can do if she is simply aware of the feminine love encrypted on her body and written into her DNA."

Mother: "And there is the difference. Men seek sex with women as a temporary remedy to dampen their fear of the void that is all around them. Having never experienced oneness with another from inside their bodies, they cannot imagine that the nothingness that is underneath and behind life and the universe is loving and nurturing and infinite in peace.

"And this is why our Order exists. Our magical takes hold of the souls of the most important men in society in order to shape the destiny of Atlantis. This is not a power play or arbitrary action on our part. It is the very nature of the feminine mysteries to surround the electrical fire in the male so as to refine, purify, and transform it.

"Otherwise, left to themselves, men would fill society with a will to power where the only purpose is to see who can rise higher and to what extent they can subdue nature laying waste to the world in the process of conquest. Without inner peace, men feel half dead and so are desperate for a brief taste of excitement that can overcome their feeling of inner numbness."

Daughter: "We have been doing this with men for 5,000 years. But everything comes to an end. Eventually they will rebel and strike out on their own. They will want to know themselves without being guided and shaped by feminine love. Isn't this so?"

Mother: "There comes a time when men and women must consciously join—we must fertilize each other in order to survive. Until a race has mastered all physical limitations and ascends, survival will always be an issue. Survival must never be taken for granted, no matter how bright the light appears to be in the souls of mankind or how noble its leaders and wise men.

"You are quite right. What we are as women we will never know or be able to imagine until men do for us what we are now doing for them. They must focus their full power upon us and unite with us from within, not in their quest for knowledge and survival. But rather for the sake of love, because love commands all beings to reach out and become one in order to transform."

Daughter: "How much time do we have?"

Mother: "Perhaps the end will come in our own generation. Men have already been born whose souls are beyond the reach of our magic. If they are lucky, they will find infinite joy when they look inside of themselves. But it is far more likely that having lost the wonder of what it is to be alive they will turn to the dark side. Instead of union with others, the desire for union will be replaced by a craving to dominate and take possession of each other."

Daughter: "Is there nothing that can be done?"

Mother: "Step outside of linear time. In another age of the world, you have already lived a life in the future in which love and power are joined. And this will come to be, for it is the only way the human race will survive."

A Meeting in the Great Library

The Great Library is underground. Each floor archives the knowledge of several thousand years of Atlantean history. There are five official floors. The first two are open to the public. The other three require permission to enter. Only a few library personnel may access all levels.

Each level also has restricted areas. There are secret archives whose location is only known to certain linage masters. And behind walls and hidden doors, there are sealed archives lost and forgotten.

Sa, one of two female members of the High Council, sits in a lounge reading on the third level. Looking at her face is like watching the sun rise, its rays filtering into a grove while the full moon sinks beneath the opposite horizon. Her beauty is dazzling and yet also soft and inviting; it surges in strength while in the same moment it is yielding—she could easily be the most beautiful woman in Atlantis if she did not disguise her physical and personal charms.

Sa senses Radea entering the room. Though the floors and wood-paneled walls are spotless, even marble decays. There is ancient dust in the air from six thousand years of library silence. In spite of this, Sa catches Radea's scent when he is thirty feet away —it reminds her of a moist field of wheat two weeks after harvest with dirt, puddles, and organic matter composting. And it is the scent of a wolverine marking his territory; even the nostrils of a bear would flair with a warning of danger.

Demons honor this man. He has a gift of power. Somewhat jaded, at times boyish, he possesses a straightforward honesty that even his enemies appreciate.

Sa knows otherwise. Radea's father was executed as a political pawn after the brief theft of the Mentarch, the most sacred artifact in Atlantis. The father covered for his son's involvement.

With that death, Radea assumed the hereditary title of Curator of the Great Library. He also became the second in command of the Dark Order, a magical society that from its beginning has been forbidden.

Radea sits down next to Sa.

Radea speaks with the voice of an old friend who always secretly wished to be her lover—tender yet holding back, "It is said that these halls are haunted by lost souls. But today, with you being here, any ghost that enters this place will find its way home. How may I assist you?

"You have closed your mind to the dreams I send. I worry about you," Sa says.

Radea replies with his boyish smile, "I am fine. I am fine. I have never been stronger or clearer in my purposes."

A thought flashes through Radea's mind—looking into Sa's eyes is like gazing at a magic mirror. You never know what thing from the present, the far past, or the distant future will gaze back at you.

Sa smiles as she catches the thought.

Radea says, "I would be a fool if I did not ask—what is it that you people do in your secret Order? We have no records, no trace, no evidence, no investigations—am I the only one in all of Atlantis who knows of your Order's existence?"

She holds his gaze silently.

Radea goes on, "I mean, look, your involvement in my life is no accident."

Sa makes a face as if to remind him that women have their own ways and necessary secrets.

Radea continues, "It is not as if I can't figure it out for myself. I know enough about secret Orders. There is nothing I cannot imagine."

Sa says, "Go ahead. Give it your best shot."

Radea responds, "The first time I met you, you were wearing ceremonial wings and virtually nude ... You saved my life and then you put me through hell. Well, it was a horrific experience with mobs of women chasing me on the Day of Rituals.

"And the words you said the next time we met: 'I can give you whatever you ask as long as you open your heart to my light.'"

Sa says, "Your conclusions?"

"You combine love and lust," Radea replies. "You push trust to its limits. And you have some gift the human race does not yet possess. You take the molten hot cauldron of desire in men; you drop into it a piece of the Philosopher's stone wrapped in wax, and the molten lead turns into golden light.

"You take not the seed of the man's body but the vision or dream within his heart and you cloak it with your beauty until it is reborn as spirit or else manifests in some remarkable way that makes the world new.

"Am I missing anything?"

"You have not addressed why we do this," Sa says.

Radea replies with confidence, "I think we share in common the same desire: to transform the world. You are doing it from the side of love. I am doing it from the side of power."

Sa responds, "And so the question is: Is power the servant of love or must love submit to power to fulfill its purposes? That is how you see it, isn't it?"

Radea replies, "Very perceptive. I wish that love were the underlying purpose of life. I really do.

"He'ad'ra and I have the same problem: at the core of my being is an emptiness that nothing can penetrate. Until love invades that desolation, I am stuck with the pursuit of power. Perhaps you would like to invade my desolation? How about tonight or why not now?" Radea invites, wishing.

Sa ignores his rudeness. "The difference between you and He'ad'ra is that he has a sense of wonder. He is in awe of the beauty of the universe. He is willing to become nothing to reflect that beauty inside of him.

"But you are clingy. No sense of wonder, no awe. For you, beauty is something to possess. You are like a star that has burned up the fuel at its core so all that is left is for it to implode upon itself. Your art is the work of destruction.

"He'ad'ra has passed through his inner darkness. For all your ancient knowledge from other ages and secret societies, you are still terrified to enter the part of yourself that is unknown and uncharted."

"Tell me," Radea asks, "what is hidden in my inner darkness?"

"My love," Sa says simply.

Radea responds, "I am the heir to twenty thousand years of research into the Mysteries. Sweet child of the Pleiades, I believe you. I really and honestly do.

"Find me again in another lifetime when I am more receptive to your beauty and I have not been dealt cards that place in my hands the fate of Atlantis."

Note: A scene from the story from the ancient civilization of Atlantis where He'ad'ra meets Le'ah'e.

In the garden of a lavish estate in Atlantis, Le'ah'e sees a hawk with claws outstretched flashing down and grasping a snake on the ground. The hawk takes to the air clutching the snake but the snake manages to wrap its body around one of the hawk's wings and the two animals flop down to the ground. The snake coils its body around both wings and the neck of the hawk now lying on its back.

Le'ah'e sees a man in work clothes bending over a plant turn around at the sound of the two animals hitting the ground. The snake rises up a foot above the hawk and, without losing its grip on the hawk, hisses furiously at the gardener. The man, He'ad'ra, walks up and kneels close enough that the snake, with the fury of hell, strikes at him repeatedly but he is just out of its reach.

Looking around, He'ad'ra reaches for a branch and pins the snake's head to the ground and then grasps the snake behind its head. Even so, the snake will not uncoil form the hawk.

He'ad'rea, with a deep, mesmeric voice, entones: "eeeee, lllll, mmmmmm."

The snake slowly, reluctantly uncoils from the hawk and crawls off through the grass. He'ad'ra' places the branch between the two claws of the hawk, still upside down. Though still stunned, the Hawk's claws close on it. He'ad'ra lifts the branch and with it the hawk off the ground.

The hawk slowly raises its head and looks into He'ad'ra's eyes and then leaps into the air. With two beats of its wings, the hawk flies up and perches on a tree limb fifty feet up.

Le'ah'e walks over to confront He'ad'ra. She says, "You violate my dreams. And now you violate my garden. Who are you?"

He'ad'ra replies, "I am not permitted to speak with you."

Le'ah'e again asks, "Who are you?"

He'ad'ra replies, "The new gardener.

Le'ah'e puts her hand out to touch his aura and says, "You are no gardener."

She steps closer and looks into his eyes. Calmly, probing, she says, "With the snake ....? You speak the language of the creator."

He'ad'ra says, "I am not ...."

Le'ah'e says, "Shut up and answer my question—Do you speak the language of the creator?

He'ad'ra replies, "Yes."

Le'ah'e demands, "Show me." She waits and then says, "And then I will go away." She goes on as she stares into his eyes, "And I won't speak to you again. Not a word."

With quiet charisma, He'ad'ra says, "The divine majesty is known for its creativity. What dream would you make real?"

Le'ah'e says, "What do you see when you look into my heart?"

He'ad'ra says as he focuses on her, "What lies within you is beyond the knowledge of our world. What you ask is too dangerous."

Le'ah'e says, "Tell me what you see."

He'ad'ra says, " I see the consort of God, the Goddess of the Earth—her spirit dwells within you."

Le'ah'e asks, "Will she appear if you call her?"

He'ad'ra replies, "Yes."

Le'ah'e says, "Call her now."

He'ad'ra says, "We have to touch."

Le'ah'e says, "Why?"

He'ad'ra replies, "Because in the divine art, there is no separation." She puts her arm around his waist and says, "Will this do?" He'ad'ra nods and then says with another voice than his own, Goddess.

Earth, air, fire and water are your children.
You are the storm and its lightning
The sea that drinks in the rain with salty lips you are the fire beneath the earth,
The deserts, the forests, the mountains, the plains
By your command
Volcanoes explode,
Dust blinds the sky
ice ages rise and fade
And by your song
Nine planets dance and sing.

Nothing happens. Le'ah'e gives He'ad'ra a look. He'ad'ra looks back at her. She sees a radiant light reflected in his eyes and across his face. The goddess of the earth appears. Le'ah'e bows down.

The goddess says as she walks toward them, "For four billion years I have watched over and tended this planet. I created life. No religion comprehends who I am, though it is I who grant permission before each appears."

Addressing Le'ah'e she says, "Your innermost desires are the same as my dreams: To have children who can see through the eyes of the stars, who unite all opposites, the constellations themselves, into one song of love.

"Will you shine with my light? Be anointed with my beauty? Speak with my voice?"

Le'ah'e says, "Yes."

"Two things I require: Establish justice on the earth and do as my Beloved and I do—make the world new."

Le'ah'e asks, "How do I do this?"

The goddess says, "Create a religion without rituals, priests, or temples in which love, wisdom, power, and justice are equally honored and pursued."

115

The goddess fades away. Le'ah'e remains staring at where the goddess stood. He'ad'ra moves slightly so that Le'ah'e's arms no longer touches him. But Le'ah'e grasps his hand and turns toward him. Tears rain down her cheeks.

Radea enters his bedroom. It is late at night. He sits at a table and then suddenly rises, holds his head, and throws himself onto his bed. A dark blue sphere of light appears in his room. An archdemon materializes within the light and then speaks to Radea. Radea isn't sure if he is dreaming.

Radea: "What do you want?"

Archdemon: "Hello."

Radea: "What is this? You happen to be in the neighborhood and drop in for a casual conversation?"

Archdemon: "Hear me out. Each race has its strengths and weaknesses. Ours has strong will but is weak on feeling. Yours has weak will but a wondrous sense of being alive."

Radea: "I rarely feel alive. More like now—like I am caught in a bad dream."

Archdemon: "It is through your soul that you feel alive. The soul contains your ability to have new experiences along with a sense of wonder and beauty. It enables you to feel happiness, peace, contentment, and satisfaction. As you begin to lose your soul, you can still experience pleasure, but not bliss and ecstasy and never rapture.

"With a soul, affection, love, and intimacy are always a possibility. Without a soul, you can only experience these things through fantasy as if you are viewing them from outside like a mirage hovering over a distant horizon.

"But if you are already in despair, feeling alienated and lost, depressed and devoid of wonder and curiosity, then you have nothing to lose. You soul has no meaning to you.

"Except for this one thing—hope. Hope is the possibility of something new coming to you. But if your despair has already led you to abandon hope and you no longer wish be made new, to change and to transform, then we can custom design a plan of exchange just right for you."

Radea: "I always thought of you demons as being narrow-minded and shallow twits. Overly possessive .... you know what I mean?"

Archdemon: "Let me refresh your memory on the part demons have been assigned to play in the unfolding of creation.

"Everyone needs a purpose to be alive. Otherwise being here in the physical world would have no meaning. And yet, oddly, there are human beings who have no purpose. They have chosen no part to play in this magnificent and wondrous universe that surrounds us. And so we demons act as spirit guides, inspiring and prompting human beings to step up and accept the great destiny that awaits them.

"The bottom line is that we do good work. Someone is confused or in despair? We grant obsessions that draw them back to their senses. We place in their soul vices so they have something inside of themselves they can strive with in order to develop courage and strength.

"If someone lacks empathy and is a virtual sociopath, we create situations in which they are deeply wronged by someone else. And though they lack any ability to feel what others' feel, instantly they will experience that most powerful of emotions— revenge. And what is revenge but a commitment to make another person feel what we feel by going through a similar experience. After all, if someone wrongs you, you can make things right, quickly and decisively. Revenge is all about establishing a gut to gut connection and making life fair.

"If someone abuses you, you get angry. That is only natural. And creating the emotion of anger is one of our specialties. Anger and rage infuse the soul with a massive amount of raw, fiery energy. And without that firsthand experience with the explosive power of fire, it is impossible for an individual to develop will power. And without will power, a species becomes extinct. You could say we demons watch over the human race to make sure you survive and prevail.

"If someone is so confused they have lost their ties to even their body and their soul is at risk of dissolving into the void, demons come to the rescue. That is why lower demons exist—to act as surrogates that take possession of the weak and implant in them blind, primordial cravings that tie them to life until they are ready to get back on their feet.

"Or if someone, even those of noble birth like yourself, are in a state of despair, why our job is to take away your freedom so that life is seen in perspective. You never appreciate what you have until it is gone. Then you realize that freedom is worth whatever price you must pay to regain it."

Radea: "You are saying malice is good?"

Archdemon: "Not malice but the results. With a little fear and old-fashioned terror in just the right amounts, people become hard working, productive, and, above all else, loyal—we establish long lasting ties to a community."

Radea: "Community?"

Archdemon: "Oh I realize the Thieves' Guild, the Assassin's Guild, or rule by a mob might not measure up to your standard of what constitutes a genuine community. But the spiritual laws governing the operation of communities are indisputable.

"It does not matter how loving a community is or how productive and helpful it is in serving others. All we require to put an end to any spiritual development of any kind in an individual is to control one of three things—either what people think, that is, their beliefs, what they feel, or their actions.

"Join a loving community where everyone cares for each other with genuine affection? It does not matter. Get them to accept without question any set of doctrines, no matter how profound, and that spiritual community now falls under demonic jurisdiction. Without freedom of thought, the heart is like a beautiful song bird imprisoned in a gilded cage."

Radea: "And I suppose assigning people to hell after they die is another one of your gifts that grant purpose to life?"

Archdemon: "No one goes to hell against their will. They die and some are so confused and lost that everywhere they look they see only fear and terror. And so the only place they feel comfortable is filled with horror and suffering. At least that is something with which they are familiar. They accept that as home.

"Like those who die in violent circumstances are unable to move on. They are obsessed with reliving the trauma of their death over and over again. Attachment to a body and a personal identity is necessary in the beginning as a way to learn and to experience life. But some are slow learners. They consider that what they are attached to is the only true reality.

"After all, no one who lives in abject poverty closes their eyes and dreams of having all their needs met, being surrounded by a loving family, and playing a productive and fulfilling role in the world. It never occurs to them that they are free to dream any dream, that for at least the time at night when they asleep they can be anyone and experience anything.

"And no one who has been violated and abused, harmed and dominated, closes their eyes at night and dreams of having an intimate, tender, and caring lover and of being surrounded by friends who are loyal and true. It just doesn't happen. People cannot imagine existing without familiar attachments no matter how horrendous those attachments are.

"All the same, we demons are not without a heart. Built into hell is an escape plan. All you need do is share with another an act of kindness and you are banished from hell forever. There is no room in hell for even one act of compassion.

"And some in hell eventually get bored of suffering and are ready to move on. There is nothing holding anyone anywhere.

"And your own saints present the best argument for how benevolent demons are. They proclaim that demons are but angels in disguise. We come to free people of their false attachments that hold them back from experiencing the best in life and the marvels of the spiritual worlds that surround us on all sides.

"I am sure you can understand this. But most people are so insecure they feel threatened by any little change in their lives. If you put off to the side all fear you become enlightened. Angels have tried to teach this to mankind but they have failed. It is left to demons to put on display every kind of fear until a man opens his eyes and realizes that it does not matter where you dwell as long as you feel free in your soul."

Radea: "Why are you even talking to me?"

Archdemon: "We have a position available and you appear qualified."

Radea: "You are pulling my leg."

Archdemon: "This is the beauty of being an archdemon. Though we often lie and deceive to bring about what we consider to be good results, in your case truth is on our side. You are so perceptive you can see through any lie. And so I can speak to you about things you already know to be true.

"The Dark Order to which you are heir does not possess enough knowledge and wisdom to fill the void inside yourself."

Radea: "I can sense that. So what?"

Archdemon: "Once or twice every thousand years your race is tested to see if there is someone who can pass through the darkness and obtain cosmic wisdom. Succeed and you shall have all that you desire."

Radea: "What about love?"

Archdemon: "Love …. Yes …. Tell me what you want from a woman?"

Radea: "I want a woman who is innocent yet sophisticated, vulnerable yet committed, vivacious and wild yet caring and tender, sensual yet perceptive. I want a woman who is so receptive that she can contain all that I am enfolding me in an instant with her eyes, her lips, her breath."

Archdemon: Leaning forward, the archdemon says, "Too easy. Try again. Try speaking from heart."

Radea: "I want a woman who I can be one with and one with the universe in the same moment. After all, what is a woman for to a man but the beauty of nature right there in front of him available to touch, to taste, and to melt into him at his command."

Archdemon: "This is what I like about you. Unlike so many others with their petty requests for wealth, fame, pleasure, and power you bring your full imagination to the bargaining table.

"Your request is granted."

The archdemon disappears.

Radea wakes. There in his bed beneath the sheets is a nude woman fast asleep. Radea cautiously raises the sheets to look at her.

Radea: "Who or what are you?"

Ga: Waking, she says, "I love you."

Radea: "I should believe this?"

Ga: "I am proof of the existence of love."

Radea: "Let's see this proof."

Ga pushes him down on the bed and begins kissing his chest moving downward.

The hall has green marble tiles on the floor. At the center of the floor is a 30-foot-wide circle of varnished rose wood. This is where the magical event takes place.

The VIP guests are arriving. Of course the high priest is here. This is the first time he will see the young woman chosen to be his consort for seven years. We might suspect that this high priest has unusual abilities. One of his skills is that he can change his brain waves so as to understand not just what others' think but how their minds work to produce their thoughts. He has mental empathy. He can see what others' see as if he is looking through their eyes. It is almost impossible to argue with him. He is always aware of the bottom line.

And there are the seven kings from the seven nations united in the kingdom of Ubarim. There is king Irkomen, the most outgoing, friendly, and dangerous. The temples in his kingdom are dedicated to the planet we call Jupiter. King Irkomen has everything you would want in a king. There is chivalry, nobility, wisdom, fairness, and generosity. The malice at the center of his heart is the one exception.

The custodian of the mermaid archives is here. She can slow time and scan the entire human race with her mind. She is so empathic she can relive other people's memories as if they are her own.

Of all who exist on earth, she is one of the most skilled in speaking with spirits. If she thinks of a spirit, almost immediately it walks through the wall into her room. You can understand why she has to cover any mirrors in the room where she sleeps. All mirrors are magical and around her spirits come out of her mirror and walk around thinking they are now material.

Of course what would Ubarim be without an agent of Saturn to weigh in on issues regarding evolution and justice? Though priests of the temple of Saturn prefer to let karma take its course, on occasion an agent of Saturn can time shift, bringing karmic results from the future into the present. This is done to accelerate the learning process.

There are unusual moments in history where amazing figures appear and meet. We saw this during the War of Independence. You had people like Madison, Hamilton, Jefferson, Washington, and Benjamin Franklin all gathered together to write the constitution for a new kind of nation.

We saw it in ancient Greece where a Socrates had a student named Plato. Plato was the source of the story of Atlantis. And Plato in turn had a student called Aristotle. Philosophers still look back at Aristotle and ask themselves, "How did he do that?" He was the first to ask questions that philosophers would ponder for thousands of years.

And Aristotle was tutor to a man who became Alexander the Great. Aristotle taught the young Alexander that you can understand anything if you put your mind to it. Alexander applied his mind to military tactics and became one of the greatest generals in history.

You get the idea. History has these moments when different streams briefly unite forming one river of life.

Oh yes, there is a young warrior priest from the temple of Mars here whose name is Hirah. You could call Hirah an agent of Mars. Perhaps Hirah should have been screened more carefully. Hirah and the woman about to dance have an unusually strong chemistry.

Now every seven years, in accordance with the rules governing the Great Rite, a new consort for the high priest is selected among all the available women in Ubarim. Call it a beauty contest in which not so much the body but the beauty of the soul is what is prized above all else.

But when it comes down to it there is only one requirement she must possess. She has to be able to channel the Goddess of the

Earth so the Goddess can be seen in living flesh as the girl dances her dance.

As you might expect, there are a lot of stories about this performance. Seven years ago the priest form the Temple of the Moon was so infatuated, obsessed .... or let us say inspired that he went to live in a cave for the next seven years in order to recover. Beauty can do that to you—if its energy accumulates into a charge like ball lightning on the one hand that makes the hair on your arm stand up; and on the other hand it is like a magnetism so cold your body may go on shivering for several days afterwards.

Call it the Odysseus effect. You remember, Odysseus had his crew tie him to the mast as they sailed by the sirens. The other crew members had wax in their ears and so could not hear. But Odysseus, who would sleep with mortal and divine women possessing special powers of enchantment, wanted to hear the siren songs for himself. He wanted to know if there is a feminine voice so skilled it can steal a man's soul with the promise of love.

Silly Odysseus. The Greeks had just besieged Troy for ten years to take Helen of Troy back who the goddess Aphrodite had given to Paris. The Greeks may have celebrated the Eleusinian Mysteries that had Demeter and Persephone at the center, but how little they understood women.

Odysseus was lucky. He survived the encounter as did the priest of the temple of the moon. Others on occasion who have witnessed the Goddess dance died a few days later. Too much beauty, like too much truth or getting too close to God, can shatter the delicate fibers that bind the soul to flesh and bone.

You could say women are at times a magic mirror. When the focus is clear, you can see in them the part of yourself that is most hidden—like a vision of your destiny or what the world will one day be. And the Goddess of the Earth—can it be said any clearer than this? The Goddess dreams that one day an intelligent race will appear on earth that, like any lover, will share her dreams—to be one with the universe.

Everyone is seated around the circumference of the circle. The young woman enters. She disrobes and begins her dance to the music she has selected.

Just a moment. I have to prepare myself when I too witness this. How do I describe her dance? Let me defer to the warrior priest Hirah whose poem describing her movements was somehow leaked to the public a few days later:

I saw a naked woman dancing a slow, hypnotic dance
In a kingdom of my imagination so far away
It is not found in any myth or religion.

Your hips rising upon the air
As a breath on a path of love
Flies on wings to the heart of God.
Your thighs circling, molded
As a sea of sand dunes sculptured by the wind
An intimate caress
My palm will never find
Flowing upon your skin.

Your hips embraced
By shadow and light
Drinking as an elixir
The secret places of your delight
I shall never taste your lips
Nor the rhythm of the sea
Flowing around your thighs
Though I drown in a sea of bliss
Though ecstasy be my wine.
Space itself curls and turns
Lost on dark pathways
Gateways Eternity can only find
Within this moment
As your body rising now descends.
Your face moving mysteriously, eyes closed
Yet lit from deep within
Whispers names
Of ancient powers men have long forgotten.

Your hands, your fingers
Adrift on the winds my soul will never know
Sail as moonlight through white winters
Sail as twilight through my dark desires.

You hum,
Your passion glistening on your skin
And your scent
Shakes me as you pierce me deep within
My nerves scream like rivers running
From the tallest mountains
Evaporating and lost
Amid the desert's red dunes
Your body pulses
The music undulating
Enchanted by your skin
My heart beats
But I cannot find the way,
My soul sleeps, a lion in his jungle
Still, I can find no rest
Even as I hear
The depths of your fullness
Releasing in your breath
Even as your voice
Winds its way through my soul
With more intimate caress
Than a river shaping a valley
Flowing upon its hills,
Its granite cliffs, its secret pools.
There is a candle
A wick naked and exposed
It burns furiously
Inhaling the air
Exhaling flames of desire
Melting

Darkness submits
To worship upon this altar
Your body
Your hips whose play
A wine
Fermented from starry ecstasies
My craft will never find
The flame is red
The flame is white
The flame burns me
With a delight I shall never taste.

Magenta clouds at dawn strung out
As islands across a sea
As a necklace around your neck
The Lord of the Winds
With his soft, moist kiss
Searches for your breasts
With a devouring hunger
The Lord of Light
Casts his rays
Into the sea of my sorrow
And borrows my eyes
To watch you dance
And weeps at twilight
For the sweetness
My lips will never taste.

Your hair drops upon your shoulders
Flies around your neck
The flowing, rippling, shimmering
Of water in a falls
Of smoke swirling in the wind
Are not as wet
Are not as dry

As your hair
Which burns, and freezes, and impales me
With promises of what might have been
Had we met
And you gave your love to me
Its waves of bliss
Its familiarity
Your hair like rain
Falling upon my face.

I have entered a place
Where men are forbidden to go
A place of the soul
A wilderness unknown
Where breath cannot flow
The heart cannot seek
But it is clearly seen as you dance—
Your hips and thighs
Caressing the air
Your body sharing your innermost being
Unfolding as you enfold this moment
In circles, curls, and turns
Rising and descending
With a love I shall never know.

If I could dance with you
If I could walk upon the wind
If I could bargain with the stars
For breath to float my sails
If I could sail through every dream
As a sailor every sea
And you are the sound of the sea
When I am lost and lonely
Guiding me by the light of stars
The moon's silvery touch upon my skin

Igniting me within
As golden fires without limit
Stumble intoxicated through the sky
Having spied upon our love.

Come dance with me
I will be your consort, your guide, your soul, your love
As you sing
The winds of eternity run their fingers through your hair—
Once we held hands by a well so long ago
Your smile rode above the waves
Like a bird migrating across countless lifetimes
To return to me again
And again, your soul, your song revives me
As I sink into your heart
And sleep and rest and dream
As you caress my skin.

Part IV
Creation Stories

And seven mighty angels, lords of creation, stood before the throne of the Creator. And the Creator spoke and said, "What part will each of you play in fulfilling my will to create the universe?"

And the first angel came forth and spoke with the voice of a great void filled with cosmic explosions, "I shall create the sky and an array of stars and galaxies that light might shine. Thereby a trace of your glory and joy shall echo through the universe till the end of time."

And the second angel came forth and spoke with a voice of thunder and a roar of winds across great waters, "I shall create the planets and worlds dividing the waters from the dry land so that order might rise from chaos. Mountains and seas, hills and streams, volcanoes and trees, clouds flowing, lightning striking—all of these shall I call into being that the firmament might bear witness to the notes with which your voice sings."

And then the third angel spoke with the voice of wonder, "I shall bring life into being on many planets within the galaxies. All manner of creatures I shall design that life might come to know itself as one gazes into another's eyes."

And the fourth angel spoke with a voice of truth, radiant and dazzling in light, "I shall grant these creatures intelligence that they choose their own paths in life. Over the course of time, they shall guide and refine nature until it attains perfection."

And the fifth angel spoke with a voice of longing and hope, "I shall send dreams of what can be. Thereby ideals shall appear even in the darkest place so that all creatures shall taste and share our ecstasy."

And the sixth angel spoke with a calm and detached voice, "I shall place within the minds of living beings a mirror so clear, a wisdom so vast, the stars, planets, galaxies, and all that exists shall be reflected within it in perfect clarity. In this way, those who desire shall attain perfect enlightenment and absolute freedom."

The seventh angel waited a moment, meditating quietly to herself on what within the Creator's will was left undone. She then came forth and spoke with the voice so pure and kind that it drew together and entwined all other voices within it.

She said, "I shall create love of such depth that those who are touched by it shall hold in their hearts the entire universe and every being nurturing, healing, and fulfilling each. Thereby, in the fullness of time, living beings shall unite all creatures, planets, stars, and angelic powers into one song—love and beauty joined. Then and only then will your will to create the universe be done."

An angelic being was speaking with the Creator. And he says, "I am not quite sure I understand your plan. I already possess a body of light. Bliss overflows from the depths of my heart. My joy is boundless and I am united to every being that loves throughout the universe.

"Why then have you set before me a quest that will take me into the depths of darkest matter? What more can I be than what I already am?"

And the Creator replies, "What I am asking you to do is quite simple. Put aside your light, your wisdom that shines so bright, your bliss and boundless happiness, your ecstasy of oneness with so many others—put it all off to the side for a little while.

"In this way, you will be able to be born as a human being in a realm of linear time where consciousness is shaped by weight, density, and form. You will then attain self-awareness under situations and circumstances you do not control. And you will grow through your interactions with others who will be quite different from you.

"Slowly over many life times you will increase in experience until one day you shall finally ascend and stand right here before me again. This is the only way that the true glory and beauty of the universe can be displayed.

"But you will not be alone. Wonder shall be your guide. Beauty shall be your inspiration. And as always wherever there is love I shall be there walking by your side."

And the angelic being asks, "I have a question if it is permitted?"

The Creator says, "Sure. Go ahead."

The angelic being asks, "What if I get lost and fail to ascend? The world where you are placing me carries a high level of difficulty not to mention separation. The isolation is beyond what I can imagine and I have an incredibly good imagination."

The Creator replies, "Day unto day and night unto night the physical universe declares my glory—in the sea you can perceive my love; the blue sky is an image of my mind; the starry sky by night—right there in that vastness—witness the depths of my heart; and the trees, mountains, forests, and plains are expressions of my art.

"All you will need to do in case you lose your way is to focus on your five senses. Behold the universe surrounding you, for hidden in nature and in your sensory perceptions are all the secrets of creation."

And the angelic being says, "I get it—I am to become my own creation.

And the Creator who dwells within an infinite void replies, "Ah. There. What you have just said cannot be stated more clearly. Now then be off and the best of luck to you."

And seven mighty angels, lords of creation, stood before the throne of the Creator. And their spokesman steps forward and says, "Almighty, maker of heaven and earth, you who are beyond all understanding, ineffable and shrouded in mystery; you for whom all the stars and galaxies are but a faint echo of your joy and glory, hear our petition.

"We have a problem that resists solution. It interferes with our commission to bless all beings, to insure their lives are fulfilled, to grant them opportunities to attain to their highest paths in life, and to decide what part they wish to play in the unfolding of the universe."

The Creator says, "Go on."

The angel explains, "The problem is that some convert the blessing we give them to a dark purpose. We give the ability to understand others and to negotiate fair and just agreements, but this gift only makes them arrogant. They use their heightened insight to dominate and to make others' choices for them. They feel the gifts they are given are owed to them and that they should have been given more right from the start.

"If we offer them wealth and abundance, they waste it on selfish pursuits. If we give them the ability to love, they use their empathy to enchant others so they submit to them. If we give them purposes to fulfill that produce things of value that endure through all ages of the world they produce instead weapons of war. There is no end to their greed. They live as if their will is the only thing that is real. They set aside no time to celebrate the divine, the beauty of the universe, or the joy of being alive.

"Consequently, our attempts to bless them and to fulfill their lives result in failure. We humbly ask for a few suggestions."

And the Creator, who sits upon a throne that exists neither in space nor in time but rather is beyond, replies, "Did I not create the blue sky?"

And the angel replies, "Yes, you did."

And the Creator asks, "Why did I do so? I could have left above the earth darkness and clouds of dust and ash, or else impenetrable mists of sulfur and acids."

And the angel replies, "You created the sky by day so that in one single glance men might see that regardless of the raging storms of life, regardless of being surrounded by death on all sides, and regardless of the horrors that pursue them from the moment they are born, the mind itself is open, pure, and clear."

"Is that it?" asks the Creator with a tone of voice implying the angel is missing the main point.

And angel, good at improvisation, replies, "And, in contemplating the sky that embodies freedom and the enlightened mind, there shall come a time when each man shall find the universe reflected inside of him."

And the Creator asks, "Did I not create the sky by night filled with countless stars?"

And the angel replies, "Yes."

And the Creator asks, "Why?"

And the angel replies, "So that in one single glance men might perceive that the mind is infinite."

The Creator says, "And?"

The angel replies, "And if they persist in contemplation, perceiving without thoughts intervening, they shall sense a great stillness embracing the universe in which the beginnings and ends of all things are united in peace and harmony.

And the Creator asks, "Did I not create the oceans and the seas encircling the earth?"

And the angel says, "Yes, you did."

And the Creator asks, "Why do you suppose I did so? I mean, I could have placed the earth outside the goldilocks zone so that it was either too hot or too cold to have liquid water on its surface encircling the planet."

And the angel says, "So that in one single glance men might behold in front of them extending from horizon to horizon a love that has nurtured life on earth for billions of years. In its very essence it gives without asking for anything in return. All embracing and with infinite receptivity, it seeks to fulfill any being's deepest dreams and the visions hidden within their hearts."

And the Creator asks, "How is that going?"

And the angel replies, "Not good. They glance a lot at the sea but the love that it embodies is not yet one of their discoveries."

And the Creator asks, "Why do you suppose that is?"

And the angel replies, "When they can create love through force of concentration so that it emanates from their own bodies filling the space around them for miles, then truly they will awaken and perceive that the oceans of the earth and the sun that shines down upon it emanate a love that extends to the ends of the universe."

And the Creator asks, "Did I not create mountains, trees, forests, plants, hills, and plains?"

And the angel replies, "Yes."

And the Creator says, "Why would I bother to do that? Does it not strike you that the earth with its material forms that change and fade away are separate from what is celestial and spiritual and so not worthy of serious attention or investigation?"

And the angel replies, "You created matter in its densest form so that men might have material to build a home where love, light, and life are celebrated in the ordinary moments of the day when they gather to eat, share, and sleep."

And the Creator says, "There must be more to it than that."

The angel responds, "Lightning is in the heartbeat, winds in the breath, seas in the bloodstream, minerals and the densest matter are part of the body supporting and sustaining consciousness. By being aware of the physical body, they shall realize that the forces unfolding the universe are within and a part of them."

And the Creator asks, "Why did I create a void so empty the density is less than one hydrogen atom per cubic meter and the temperature is just above absolute zero?"

And the angel responds, "So that any intelligent being in one glance at this darkness that lies between the stars might comprehend what it is to be absolutely and totally receptive—to be consciousness without form or image, without space or time to give it definition."

The Creator says, "And?"

The angel replies, "And, in that moment of complete detachment, to perceive the infinite possibilities that surround us. In so doing, to create something worthy, something glorious and magnificent filled with awe and wonder, as a small token of appreciation for the beauty of the universe in which we exist.

The Creator asks, "Anything else going on here with this void?"

And angel replies, "Yes. When things go wrong each being that possesses intelligence and consciousness might know how to return to the beginning and in so doing to restore life to what it is meant to be."

And God said, "Why have I commissioned you to bless men?"

And the angel replies, "Because it is the essence of your being to bless all things, to see that life is fulfilled in every conceivable way. You offer men the opportunity to choose a destiny so they become like you possessing the ability to make all things new."

And then the Creator says, "Now what would you suppose might be the best thing to do if when you bless men your blessings they refuse?"

And the angels replies, "Take away one by one the things they have until they reach the point where they are grateful simply to be alive and to have little things—like heartbeat, breath, their five senses, their ability to feel, to think, to love, and to share. Then they will be ready to begin again their lives without corrupting the deepest purposes of life."

And the angels asks, "But if they still refuse choosing to persist in their desire to dominate and harm others, what then?"

And the Creator says, "Then give them what I myself am: an infinite void that can create an entire universe in order to share love and that is equally content in being absolutely nothing."

"Let them then make their own choice whether they wish to be like me—nothing at all—or else to discover everything life can be.

"The creative void that I am is within every sense perception, every form of substance and energy, and in every thought and feeling. There is no end to my being or my originality.

"As I have always said and which the planets and constellations proclaim, 'Life is a gift. Use it well. Satisfy your desires and meet your needs. Fulfill your dreams. But for each man there shall come a day of reckoning—through the choices he makes he shall shape his fate, whether to create without limitation or give his attention to his ego which is destined to fade.'"

And the angel asks, "Is this confrontation with the consequences of their actions something we should make happen sooner or later?"

And the Creator says, "Use your own discretion. Sometimes to solve a problem you have to create an original solution. But my suggestion to you is that when it comes to learning from experience, sooner is better than later.

"One other thing. Encourage them to ask the right questions as I have encouraged you."

There was once a woman who complained to God. She said to him, "There is something horrible about life here on earth. It is as if you have run an experiment and the results turned out wrong. What can be done?"

And God, the almighty, the creator of heaven and earth, ineffable, unknowable, and forever beyond all comprehension, replies to her, "Yes. I have had those very thoughts myself. But I will tell you what. I have a job opening for a prophet. He will hear my own thoughts before I speak them. Will you play this role for me?"

And the woman replies, "No. Such a prophet, though seeing clearly the future and speaking with your voice—such a prophet will in no way clarify human choice. Humans shall run after false gods and continue to do terrible things to each other."

And God, the almighty, then says to the woman, "Well then. I have a second job position. I require a mighty prophet to perform miracles and to display terrifying wonders to liberate a people. In this way, history shall record that I intervene in human affairs so that justice appears on earth."

And the woman replies, "No. That will not suffice. Miracles, mighty wonders, and such will not change human nature. It will impress for a time no doubt but then it shall be treated as past acts that do not carry over to the present. In spite of your best efforts to exhort and to edify, men will continue to abuse each other.

And God, the creator of heaven and earth, says to the woman, "You know, I have a third job opening. I need a great king, wise beyond all understanding. I shall authorize him to build my house on earth so that people from all nations might come and draw close to me. I shall appear there each year according to carefully defined rituals overseen by a high priest. What do you say to that?"

And the woman replies, "No. Absolutely not. High priests with their genetic purity and their sacred rites will in no way change human nature one iota. Nations and civilizations will continue to rise and fall. Men will wage wars and even during times of peace they will continue to dominate and abuse women.

"And far worse—women will deny the divine feminine hidden within them. By turning away from their receptive grace, they will succeed in imitating men at the expense of abandoning kindness and tenderness. Without the inner union of the male and female, no liberation can be attained."

And God, the ineffable, unknowable, and forever incomprehensible, says to the woman, "You know, I am not without a plan B. I have decreed—life shall be filled with surprises.

"Consider this task I set before you to accomplish: Would you be willing to walk the earth as I myself might walk if I were in human form? Shine with my light. Speak with my voice. Do mighty deeds. Reveal wisdom on many levels by speaking in parables and telling stories that anyone can understand. Your deeds shall be recorded and passed down through the ages. All who truly listen shall know that I can be found within each heart."

And the woman, who is not completely stupid, replies to God who in his very being is called Generosity, "No. That will not suffice. Men will take your light and commit the most hideous evil so much so that the archdemons will say to themselves, 'Look at that! We must make haste and get down to earth so that we can apprentice to these human beings, for they do evil in new ways that we ourselves cannot imagine.'"

And then God finally says to the woman, "Well then, can you tell me straight out what you want?"

And the woman replies, "I cannot yet grasp it though I can feel it within my heart."

And God says, "Though I am invisible and without form or image, the voice at the core of your being speaks plainly to me. It says, 'Let me be your Presence on earth without need of temple or priest, without religion, doctrine, or ritual.'"

And the woman responds, "Yes. That will satisfy me. With each person I meet, I shall reveal from the core of their being the wonder of creation, the infinite possibilities and endless opportunities that surround them in each moment. My presence will dissolve the evil and malice of anyone who comes near to me. In this way, gradually, humanity shall be utterly transformed."

And then the woman asks, "But what am I now if I am not prophet, priest, seer, or king?"

And God replies, "I shall call you Shekinah, for you are the angel of my presence on earth."

Seizing a better hold as he wrestles with the angel, balanced, poised, muscles flexed, teeth clenched, Jacob speaks, his jaw next to the angel's ear,

"What is it like to dwell in a body made of divine fire, its radiance so penetrating the mountains and seas are transparent and the stars are no more distant from you than my hands upon your skin in this moment?

"What is it to have eyes that see through the ages—the gates of all realms stand open before your gaze so nothing is hidden anywhere in creation? What is it to have hands so luminous the Divine turns to you to accomplish its will?

"And tell me, when you love, what is it like to love when your love arises from a sea of infinite bliss so every abyss is filled and darkness is forever banished from your vision?"

And the angel replies, "I will share with you my essence if you can sustain your hold upon me, for I am not permitted to keep even one secret from those who master themselves. I am the perfection of concentration so great the elements of nature obey when I speak. Earth, air, water, and fire respond to my will my every desire to fulfill.

"You may think such power beyond belief or imagination but I do not act in isolation as one wanting to make himself great to demonstrate his power over fate. When I meditate I am joined to every being who loves throughout the entire universe. With both mortals and divine I join my heart and mind. And like many others, I guard and guide all paths of wisdom and all evolutions. And in our celebration our joy is so great there is no longer any separation between the Light we embrace and the love within our hearts.

"You may think only an angel may speak thus but I tell you with words of prophecy and with a voice of thunder and a tongue of divine fire, if you strive and abide with me through all watches of this night until dawn's first light you shall discover that I, with all my power, am but a small part of what is hidden within your own heart."

Jacob says, "You speak of a mystery beyond the power of belief. It is more than what I seek."

"Oh Jacob," the angel says, "The seed that dreams of spring sleeping in silence beneath the earth knows not that spring is already within its heart as is the soil, the wind, the rain, the earth, and the star that calls out: 'Arise and come forth.'

"But form and limitation have been created that the seed in growing into a tree might one day understand its journey; as water, minerals, light, and air revive and renew its being it shall perceive when the time is ripe that life has no end and that form is but the shell where spirit dwells.

"Then it shall send its roots down into eternity and release upon the wind seeds giving birth to new worlds, new dreams, and new destinies.

The soul unfolds, blossoming in due season, until its beauty shines so bright its light transforms the world.

"Jacob, behold! I hold in my hands the twelve fruits of the Tree of Life that are for the healing of the nations. Take them from me if you can!"

Then Jacob puts forth all his might with a mind like steel and a will as sharp as a diamond knife to pierce the heart of the angel and to steal what has been concealed from mankind for ages. And, for a moment, Jacob accomplishes his goal—

Jacob's eyes become the angel's, his hands bright like the sun, their hearts merge and with the angel's body he is one. Then Jacob sees what the angel's light was created both to conceal and to reveal: a love of such magnitude the entire multitude of heavenly choirs falter and fail, their voices silenced before its magnificence.

Then Jacob asks, "Is there a human being in all the world who has the strength, the power, or the heart to persist in a vision such as this, to bring a small part back to the earth that it might be shared and celebrated forever by those who love?"

And angel replies, "If this is your wish I shall grant it to you, for now the sun is about to rise and eternity commands me to return home." And then the angel says with a voice of thunder resonate and tender like Gabriel's and vibrant and mighty like Michael's,

"For a thousand years prophets shall appear in every generation among your descendants. The history of the world shall revolve around your will. Nations shall rise and fall. Empires ascend and then end. And though some will twist and bend the truth to serve their own purposes those who read the signs shall find a pathway to the divine as you have found mine."

Then Jacob says, "Wait! One last request before you go, one last question still burns within my soul. You who are everywhere and from whom nothing is hidden, your voice a billion stars shouting with delight, will you wrestle with me again another night?"

The angel gazes into Jacob's eyes and replies, "The words I have spoken are not for you alone. If the human race is to survive and thrive, then let each generation designate at least one like you who has the will and the strength to wrestle with me for a blessing on another night."

BALAAM—THE GENTILE PROPHET

Moses led his people to encamp on the plains of Moab on the east side of the Jordan River by Jericho. Balak, king of the Moabites, saw how the Israelites defeated Sihon, king of the Amorites, and Og, king of Bashan. Shaken by fear, Balak sought to insure the survival of his people by consulting with Balaam.

Balaam's reputation as a prophet was already well-established. It was known to a number of kings that Balaam's powers were such that he could speak with God and gain God's counsel and assistance. And, by virtue of this ability and Balaam's magical power of trance, whatever nation Balaam blessed would be blessed and whatever nation he cursed would be cursed.

And so the elders and princes of Moab and of Midian came and offered treasures to Balaam relaying king Balak's message, "Curse for me the people of Israel that I may defeat them and drive them from my land." And when Balaam heard these words, he told the elders and princes to wait one night while he spoke with God.

That night Balaam asked God to curse the Israelites. But God told Balaam not to curse the Israelites for they were blessed. Balaam passed God's words to the messengers from Balak. When Balak received word of what had occurred, he thought, "I shall increase my offer."

Then Balak sent princes of higher rank to beseech Balaam for his assistance against Israel saying Balak would give Balaam great honor and do whatever Balaam asked of him. Again Balaam spoke with God during the night. But God impressed upon Balaam the glorious destiny of Israel and showed him visions of what was to be. In the morning, Balaam said to the princes that even if Balak were to offer him a palace full of gold and silver he could not alter Israel's destiny.

When Balak heard this, he went himself to speak with Balaam. Now as the story goes, Balaam happened to be traveling down a road and an angel with a sword was waiting in the center of the road to slay him. Balaam survives this encounter with the help of his donkey that speaks to Balaam. Permitted to continue, Balaam meets with Balak.

Twice more Balak beseeches Balaam to intercede with God. Balak takes Balaam up upon the hills, first to a place of Baal and then the top of Mount Peor. Each time seven altars were built and sacrifices made of rams and bullocks. And twice Balaam beseeches God on behalf of king Balak, but the results are always the same.

Even in the presence of King Balak, when Balaam opens his mouth to curse Israel this blessing comes forth:

"How lovely are your tents, O Jacob! Your dwellings, O Israel! Like valleys that stretch out, like gardens by the riverside, like aloes planted by the Lord, like cedars beside the waters."

In the end, in spite of their best efforts, the kings of Moab and Midian and Balaam fall to Israelite swords. And yet we might ask —Who was this gentile prophet and how was he able to speak so easily with God when over the course of millennia so few men on earth were able to do so?

Twenty years earlier, Balaam prophesied the future of a newborn child to a princess of Midian who was called Mirah. He told her that everywhere her child turned his face he would find wealth and happiness. But later, according to the decree of fate, his life would suddenly be cut off. She thanked him accepting his words and honoring his vision.

And then, as Mirah held his hand and gazed into his eyes, she asks Balaam a question no one else during his life would ask—no one else would ever presume such intimacy: "Balaam, from whence do your powers arise? What winds of spirit brush the waters of your heart with lips of inspiration or bid your soul drink such wine of vision that even the veils of the future are rent in two when you gaze upon their dark tapestry?"

151

Balaam replies, "As long as I can remember, I had been asking myself, 'What spirit, what hand, what mind, what soul gave birth to the wonders of the universe? The tree from the seed—what soul is so passionate to have envisioned and engendered this thing? The mountains from the sand—what mind has the endurance to withstand such silence and to exercise such power of command?

"'The clouds from the sky—from whose breath do the winds arise? The sun, moon, and stars—what Joy is so great that celestial light leaves but a trace of its glorious face? And of mankind—all that drives and motivates, all dreams and visions, all desires and needs—what spirit could have created such a being?'

"And so, to the tree, the mountain, the clouds, the sun, moon, and stars—I opened myself to them until I could feel the heart that gave birth to their existence.

"In all my contemplations upon all that the five senses reveal, I have searched for the source to which all of nature and life testify. And this source is named God who chooses to reveal Himself as the first light appearing from out of the unmanifest.

"One morning before the sun rose, I had finished my meditations and was having tangerines and tea for breakfast. But then the air in my room grew thick as if pregnant with some great mystery about to be born. And then, though my eyes remained open, the room ceased to exist. I looked about myself and saw that I was in an immense, clear space and yet also solid and glittering with different colors like an opal. Time and space dissolved. I could see the future and the past and any place on earth that I desired to gaze upon.

"I remained in this trance for hours not moving. And then I entered a place in which there was only nothingness—no world, no stars or sky, no thing the five senses could perceive or the mind analyze. And there, as an abyss appearing in front of me, empty, dark, without beginning or end, and yet containing all of time and space, all of life, all destinies within it, God appeared to me and spoke as clearly to me as you speak to me now."

The princess removes her hand from Balaam's and says, "Balaam, your words frighten me. I am shaken. Your words are like acid dissolving my contentment.

"How can you survive entering a temple that has no doors or windows, no ceiling or floor, no altar, and no image of God? Does the body know how to let go of its form and become more thin than wind, more pure than light? And how can your return to the land of the living after having such a vision in which all things cease to exist?"

Balaam replies, "I have trained my mind to enter the heart of the mountain and put on its robes of silence and stillness. I have entered into minerals, gems, and stones. I have learned from iron its fierce patience and rugged endurance. I can see through the eyes of the lion and the hawk surrenders its will to mine when I gaze into its eyes.

"Do not be afraid of my words. God does not come to me uninvited and neither will He seek you out unless you call out to Him."

As Mirah looks into Balaam's eyes and listens to his reply, she sees not a night sky where no stars shine. Rather, she sees in his eyes a longing for love he is unable to satisfy.

She says, "Balaam, what you are saying is that hidden within sensuality and all that the senses perceive is a secret path leading into the Divine Presence. All wonder and beauty, all that men desire, all that the diverse creatures of nature need, all of this speaks of the ecstasy from which the world has been formed. And yet I do not see this love within your heart. Balaam, would you not be a sacred chalice, an oasis here on earth, from which others may drink, be healed, and fulfill their paths of life?"

And Balaam answers, "Though I have a knack for wisdom and prophecy, a skill which few can match, love has not touched my life. I hear the birds sing. I see the trees blossom in spring. I taste the fruit the seasons produce and the beauty of the earth speaks to me continuously. But in all that I have accomplished, in all my searching, solitude has been my one and only loyal companion. I cannot even imagine what it would be like to have another who is there for me sharing heart to heart."

And so ends our story. For Balaam, altering a nation's destiny was like looking at a garden and seeing what seeds are present and the way they are planted. You need only pull a few weeds in the right places while you water and fertilize what you wish to flourish. Changing the future, when you know what forces are in play, is as simple as a prince at court, on his own initiative, whispering the right words at the right time into the right ears.

And yet when it comes to drawing close to another, to creating a dream in which two become one, Balaam was no prophet. Perceiving the destiny of nations, he failed to see how to love another with all of his heart.

And it came to pass that the Creator calls the archangel Michael to appear before His throne. And the Creator says to him, "It is a time of reckoning. Go to the planet earth and determine what part Neanderthal has chosen to play in the unfolding of the universe."

"It shall be done," replies the archangel Michael with that divine fervor and prophetic perception archangels possess in no small measure.

And straight forth without delay the archangel departs from the celestial domain. Descending and crossing through the gates dividing spirit and the outer worlds of form, he approaches the earth. Like a blaze of light, like a second sun determined to destroy darkness and night, he comes down. But as his feet step upon the ground, the archangel hides his glorious form. He dials his countenance down so that it does not blind those who are near. He wishes to observe and to measure the earth's inhabitants silently, quietly, without himself being observed.

And so the archangel focuses his gaze upon the minds and souls of every member of Neanderthal's race. Neanderthal, the archangel notices, is different from animals. Neanderthal is remarkably detached like pilgrims on a sacred quest who no longer follow a path. Nothing in their environment captures their attention. It is as if a great and noble race was placed precisely on that planet where they could not flourish, where the motivation and desire to master the world and know the self have been lost or forgotten.

For a little while, the archangel Michael sends his mind into many different Neanderthals. He blends his consciousness with their own. He feels what they feel, thinks what they think, and walks with them, hunting, gathering, eating, and sleeping at night. He tastes water with their tongues and catches the scent of bear. He eats berries from a bush and notices how they can distinguish twenty-four different qualities of taste—even to the point of determining by the flavor of a fruit from a tree whether the tree has received water from rain, a water table, or underground stream.

He takes note of how some Neanderthal know how to build and engineer, but they do not construct huts out of stone, wood, or mud bricks. They do not fortify their positions against predators. They do not make traps for game which they could then leave and return another day. They take what they need for the moment as if it is an ideal to see how little work they can do to survive and to feel satisfied.

With his preliminary observations complete, archangel Michael turns his thoughts to the question at the center of his investigation, "Who among the Neanderthals has the highest wisdom, the greatest heart, and the most profound perceptions? With whom can I speak of dreams and visions and the destiny Neanderthals seek?"

And in the same moment when he has spoken these words, one Neanderthal appears before the eyes of the archangel. The greatest and wisest of all the Neanderthals is living in a cave in what will one day be called southern France not far from the Mediterranean Sea. It is the archangel's intention to enter and meet this individual within his dreams.

But this wise Neanderthal awakes from his sleep and speaks aloud, "I am happy to meet with a celestial being so magnificent. But tell me why you awaken me from my dreams? The circle of the horizon and the ocean of the sky do not bind or limit your flight. And your eyes do not require the radiance of natural light to perceive mysteries hidden far beyond the gaze of mortal sight."

"I would speak to you," replies the archangel, "of the desires in your heart and the dreams your soul might wish to fulfill. Your race has been granted peace and grace. And for two hundred thousand years you have dwelt upon the earth. And yet I find you dwelling in a cave. You live off the land, yet you explore not. You manufacture only a few physical artifacts. You cherish no art. You live the same way your fathers and mothers lived a hundred thousand years before. It has, therefore, fallen upon me to speak with you of your destiny."

The Neanderthal stands up and walks with the archangel out through the mouth of the cave. The Neanderthal raises his hand and gestures saying, "I have no need to explore, to see what is beyond yonder mountain or across the far sea. There is sufficient food in this valley to feed my family.

"As for peace, I understand the hunger that drives the hawk to strike the dove. I understand his need for fresh blood. His eyes and claws are designed for war and he cannot escape his form. The air is his home and other birds disturb the power of his throne.

"I understand the wolf's desire to command and own the land. I see in his heart his need to mark and defend the boundaries of his territory. The hunger in his belly requires struggle and strife for victory.

"And the cold serpent that slithers through the grass—I grasp why there is venom in his bite. Aroused by heat and yearning for life he cannot find in himself, he must steal from others to acquire what he needs to recapture the peace of sleep. This unending cycle of desire and gratification, this repetition of the need to find a completion that can never be is all perfectly clear to me.

"I understand and I respect these creatures but I am not as these. My senses are not slaves of their perceptions. In every moment, I am free. As long as I live on this planet, I will dwell in peace.

"As for physical artifacts—tools, weapons to protect myself, articles of clothing, buildings, the cultivation of fields, herbal remedies, vessels to carry water and containers for food—what we now have is sufficient.

"As for art, what need do we have to draw or paint upon cave walls or bark or to fashion images in stone or clay? I can close my eyes and recall with perfect clarity any animal, plant, or tree, any scene of sky, land, or sea so vivid it is as real as any dream. Yet I am fully awake within it. What work fashioned by hands can reflect even in small measure this inner power of vision and clear recollection I already command?

"You speak to me of destiny. Are you asking me to leave behind the satisfactions that are natural to my kind? Oh magnificent being, the sight in your eyes probes and searches the depths of any mystery. And the mystery in your heart is the power that resolves conflict, restoring divine order and revealing the purposes hidden within nature.

"Come. Let us reason together. Would you remake me, reshape me, place in me a new spirit until I have improved? Do you wish me to be more curious about nature and what is hidden within or behind it? Would you have me explore and adventure? Shall I fashion tools and invent machines and begin a long journey along that road which leads to technology, industry, and productivity? Would you bless me by granting me a commission to take possession and exercise dominion over the earth?

"I will now prophecy for you how it would be. If I go that way, one day those who follow me will sit in front of machines that glow with unnatural light and imitate sound and sight. And they shall do so just to ease their pain of loneliness, to find a new friend or talk with a family member who dwells on the other side of the planet.

"Don't you see? All that they struggle to attain—all that they can ever hope to command I already have. I have my family and friends who sleep beside me in a cave. I eat in their presence. We sit across from each other and talk as the flickering flames of fire dispel the night and highlight our features. Whether we hunt or gather, we do so in each other's company. We share heart to heart and embrace freely without duplicity. We know each other's moods, thoughts, and actions as well as we know our own".

The great Neanderthal then lifts his head up so his lips are near to the archangel's right ear. And then he speaks in a whisper as if he were speaking a sacred name or revealing the secret soul of his race, "When I fall asleep at night, they are near to me. I hear their stirrings, turnings, and the sounds of their breathing. Can you, for all your divine insight, understand this mystery? We share the same needs; we share the same dreams; and we live in peace.

"As long as life depends on food and drink, on breath and heartbeat, as long as the body is joined to consciousness—a better life than this—than what we have now—will not exist.

"You cannot call us to rise up and to ascend when that process requires a journey into darkness, a path which neither sun, moon, nor stars can illuminate. Though you as a divine being may require a race to satisfy this need, we are not the one you seek. My dreams are already complete. And now I bid you let me return to my sleep, for I have exhausted my desire to reason and your visions turn my soul cold."

Thus ends the conversation between the archangel Michael, sent by the Creator of the universe, and the wisest of the Neanderthals.

But this is not quite the end of the story. The Neanderthal's mate has also awakened and has overheard the conversation. And so as the archangel turns and is about to ascend, he is halted by her gentle voice.

She speaks to the archangel and says, "On occasion, I have noticed that my mate, though wise, fails to ask the right question. So, if I may, let me put it to you simply, 'What are we missing?'"

The archangel gazes upon her in astonishment—surprise is a rare occurrence for an archangel of Michael's stature and vision. For in Michael's heart, next to his love of the Creator and fulfilling his divinely appointed missions, he loves most of all a good question. And so, unable to resist, compelled by her intelligence, he replies,

"The cave, the land, the water your drink, the food you eat, the air you breathe, your body, your senses, your mind and soul—all of these things you are free to use, to form and to mold, to shape, and to recreate according to the desires within your heart. There is no limit or restriction placed upon what you may become.

"Yet it is clear to me that it is not in your heart to probe the secrets of matter and redesign and fashion them according to your will. It is not in your dreams to create and command light as hot and bright as the light of the stars, to take and hold it in the palms of your hands and to use it to fulfill new purposes born from out of your imagination. It is not in your soul to search out every secret and probe the depths of every mystery until the entire universe becomes your home."

The woman asks simply, "What will you tell the Creator when you return with your report?"

The archangel speaks honestly, "I will tell Him this: 'Neanderthal is too wise and the grace he has been granted is too great. We will need another creature, one with a smaller brain capacity, but with an insatiable curiosity. He shall look upon the world with wonder and out of his lust to know—the desire to take it, to hold it, and make it a possession of his own.

"He shall not be as free as you are of his desires. He shall be ravished by his needs and amid struggle, strife, and every imaginable craving, he shall acquire knowledge. And this shall be both his curse and his blessing, his suffering and his grace—his attempt to reconcile his passions with the beauty and the wonder of creation will lead his race to finally rise up and to attain transcendence. They shall attain the highest enlightenment that exists in the universe as well as among all celestial beings. I can see clearly now the secret purposes that anoint this planet.

"During the course of his journey, he shall master all forms of conflict and war. Every desire of every animal shall he know. Yet in the end, the powers of creation, of reconciliation, of meditation, and peace making shall be the treasures he discovers—he shall forge these abilities from out of the desires of his heart and the flame of his imagination.

"As I am the archangel empowered to defend the purity of light, so this vision is the unique and unrivaled purpose that Divine Providence will accomplish upon this planet. After the race of Neanderthals has gone, another race shall dwell upon the earth and be offered this task. In fact, many races and civilizations shall arise, as many as it takes until this purpose is fulfilled—until a civilization is born whose members have become creators who embody the mysterious form and image of their Creator. They shall take nothing for granted until the wonder and the beauty of the universe overflow from their hearts."

And though the woman understands perfectly the archangel's words, she refuses to allow them to enter her heart. Darkness, nightmares, and suffering, the insatiable desires and pain, and the horror of that loneliness that must be endured for the sake of acquiring these divine arts—this is a way she is unwilling to go. And so she is relieved when the archangel takes his light and his divine insight and departs, returning to his celestial home.

She stands there a moment after the archangel is gone. The stars shine above. An animal cries in the distance. The wind stirs through the leaves of the trees. Then she turns, takes the hand of her mate, and, entering through the mouth of the cave, they lay down again and fall asleep holding each other close.

It is fifty thousand years later and another species, Homo sapiens, begins to drive the few remaining Neanderthal away from the fertile Mediterranean basin and now Neanderthal is no more.

And the Creator, ineffable, unknowable, and forever beyond all comprehension, calls the archangel Michael before his throne. And God speaks and says, "You see over yonder that third planet from the sun out there in the wing of that obscure galaxy?"

And the archangel Michael replies, "Yes, I do. I know exactly the one you are referring to." And the Creator goes on, "You remember Neanderthal?"

The archangel Michael replies, "Why yes. I had a wonderful conversation with the wisest of that race of beings. He embodied everything Neanderthal accomplished and dreamed. And fifty thousand years later they became extinct. It would seem that when you have everything you dream the bodily form you are wearing loses its meaning and you no longer cling to life."

And the Creator says, "As once before with Neanderthal, now is a time of reckoning. There is another species that has followed Neanderthal called Homo sapiens. Go forth now and see what part Homo sapiens has chosen to play in the unfolding of the universe. See if like Neanderthal they have satisfied themselves and attained all that they dreamed."

And Michael replies, "I stand ever ready to serve. Your will is my command."

And an instant later, Michael is there upon that planet, his feet dropping down to the ground. And in another instant, he searches through all minds that exist upon the earth and finds one individual that can speak on behalf of and for the human race.

And appearing before him, the angels says, "I am the archangel Michael commissioned by the Creator to determine the fate and destiny of your race. Therefore, answer my question: What part has Homo sapiens chosen to play in the unfolding of the universe?"

The man says calmly to the archangel, "I can only speak for myself, though obviously you can take my answer any way you want. When I was young, during the worst moments of my life and possessed by a dark vision, no one came to rescue me. No spirit guide comforted me. It was only later on after I had made an absolute commitment to the light that I was offered visions of how to fulfill what I had found within my heart.

"But the darkness was also a gift. The silent winter of the soul that I survived spoke to me. Its voice said, 'This is your time to discover the truth of the universe as it appears to you. The procedures you follow, the paths you take, and even the description of what you seek must come from your own heart. No other way guarantees the best results.'

"Furthermore, others had already gone before. Their stories, gospels, and wisdom clearly state, 'That we surrendered all attachment and passed through the extremes of abandonment is obvious—nearly impossible to miss—to anyone who reads the stories of our lives in the sacred texts set down for all time.'

"The silence I endured at that time, the loneliness, and darkness I entered, were given to me to fulfill a sacred purpose. To enter the presence of the Creator is also to stand within a place that has no definition. It has no boundaries, no forms, and there are no images to support the imagination. In order to embrace the highest light it is necessary to pass through the darkness inside oneself But darkness cannot contain a heart that loves or a spirit that is free."

The archangel presses him, "You see, your planet is most peculiar. It has been designed as a maze, a labyrinth, a testing ground, an arena, and place of ordeal. The darkness and loneliness of which you speak are hidden in the hearts of every human being. Tell me what it is you have found within your heart?"

And the man replies, "There is a love that holds the universe in its embrace. Every other kind and aspect of love is found within it.

It is in the wind whose voice and wings

Embrace the cells within our bodies
And the shoulders of the mountains.

It is in the oceans, the rain, the rivers
Whose songs of grace and receptive life
Sail through our dreams
And touch the secret chambers of our hearts.

It is in the Earth—
She whose silence shelters and protects us
Until we are ready to assume our roles
As guides, guardians, and creators of life.

It is in fire whose dazzling force and power
Binds the universe with its might
And guides our wills as we chart our courses through life.

It originates in the stillness
At the center of the heart
Where all fear is banished—
It overcomes all time and space
Renewing itself without end

"It is an absolute contentment in which the inner self is one with the universe. It is a peace so deep it is as a sea that has no shores and as a stream that flows from the dawn of time to the ends of eternity.

"For every dream that can be dreamed, it offers a time and place of complete fulfillment and absolute satisfaction.

"All affection, gentleness, tenderness, and kindness are its expressions. And yet, omnipotent and absolute sovereign in its power, the fires in the stars ignite from out of its wonder, beauty, and ecstasy. I tell you, the universe is on the verge of exploding because of the joy it contains.

"Irresistible in attraction, every desire originates from it and is satisfied through it. Revealing what is missing from life, it makes people fully alive enabling them to feel whole and complete.

"There is no vice it cannot twist or bend and make again into its opposite virtue. There is no compulsion or obsession it cannot so fill with light it becomes kind and bright. There is no ill will or malice it cannot convert into chivalry or true nobility.

"There is no crunch or karmic bind, no evil intent or design, it cannot refine into contentment and absolute satisfaction. There is no suffering it cannot so enfold within its palms, spit on, blow upon, and recreate as beauty hidden in the heart of life.

"It is the essence of all that is miraculous—shapeshifting both linear and non-linear time, it creates worlds enough so that each person can experience life to discover for himself what he wishes to be that fulfills his deepest dreams. It can pack into one moment enough wonder and beauty that it creates an eternity of destinies.

"This love is empathic, uniting, receptive, enticing, and inviting. It enables one person to know another's experiences as if they are his own."

And Michael says, "I see where you are taking this. There is a slight problem, however. It appears to be your intent to construct a new purpose for the human race. And so I am required to ask about your intentions.

"'By what authority do you intervene to create justice where there is none, peace where there is war, and to set every soul free. In fact, you intend to set an example down through the ages to other races in this galaxy of how to mediate every conflict and resolve any dispute.

"You are unleashing a love on earth that contains one of the original powers of creation that can annihilate every obstacle, barrier, and obstruction that separate one from another. From where does your inspiration arise?"

The man replies, "When I listen, I can hear the song of every star in this galaxy. And further, beyond this wondrous, whirling, living being that is our galaxy, I can hear the song of every galaxy in the universe. The beauty is incomprehensible. By comparison, my contribution to the human race is next to nothing. It is the least I can do."

The archangel Michael unfurls his wings and is about to ascend. But the consort of the man whispers to the angel from a distance. Michael hears, halts his action, and turns to her. She says, "What will you tell the Creator about the part the human race has chosen to play in the unfolding of the universe?"

And Michael replies, "If there are but one or two who are willing to pursue the divine arts without restraint, then the light that shines from them, like seeds, shall inspire and spread until your entire race ascends. This love that creates peace, the work of reconciliation that unites hearts, is one of the highest of the divine arts. It ranks among the original purposes for which this universe was created. The two of you, by becoming one, bear witness to these truths."

And then, having found the answer to his questions, the archangel turns away, rises into the sky, and, crossing the threshold separating the worlds of form from those of spirit, he disappears from mortal sight.

And after a period of linear time, the angel returned to the Creator's presence as the Creator had prophesied he would do.

And the Creator says to the angel, "How was your journey into the darkness, separation, suffering, and that abyss of loneliness that is at the heart of the human experience?"

And the angel replies, "There were many times when I thought I was lost. It was so bad that knowing I could still feel despair was the only evidence I was still alive."

The Creator continues his debriefing of the angel, "And have you accomplished the mission I set before you?"

"Yes I have," replies the angel. "As you gaze upon me you see a being who in this moment holds within his consciousness without error or distortion every single experience of every human being on earth from the beginning of that species until its final end when they left behind their human form."

"Well done," says the Creator. "I am glad someone finally understands one of the reasons I created the universe.

"Now then, are you ready for your next assignment or would you like to take a few million or a billion years off to explore the universe or oversee your own planetary evolutions?"

The angel replies, "I stand ready to serve."

"Good. Good," responds the Creator. "I wish you now to go forth and to find others in various galaxies who are on the verge of accomplishing what you have done. Show them what is possible once they have attained perfect empathy and have joined their consciousness to every other being in their racial evolution."

And the angel asks, "I am not sure I will know what is possible for them."

The Creator responds, "Then that shall be your assignment— go forth and guide and inspire others to become like me—infinite in possibilities and endless in love and empathy. Report back as before when you are done."

And the angel says, "Would you like to suggest with what race of beings I should begin or what time frame I should work in?"

And the Creator says to the angel, "Use your own discretion. Creativity is everything."

Part V

Science Fiction

Some say she betrayed us. Others say she saved us. But everyone agrees she changed our world forever.

The Tir'i'ha came through a star gate from another planet, dimension, or time—we did not know which. At first it was chaos. We tried to communicate. They ignored us. There were violent confrontations. We had no chance. None of our defenses or countermeasures worked against them.

Then a priestess, Iona, somehow established communication with the Tir'i'ha. They invited her into their little settlement that had no walls and yet no weapon we possessed could penetrate it. A month later she returned to us. She organized formal meetings and laid out a set of protocols through which our two races could interact, trade, and come to understand each other. It was an astonishing breakthrough.

We have a classless society in one sense only. If someone is gifted, he or she can rise to the highest levels of power. And this is remarkable, because social standing and rank are determined by your caste.

But in spite of our rigid social structure, we made it a priority to identify individuals with high potential when they are still children. We train them as specialists in solving problems—energy, science, health, transportation, education, art, music, entertainment, and government. We have eliminated wars because of our understanding of conflict resolution and negotiation.

But one guild trains individuals who are born with the capacity to tackle problems that have no precedent. Their minds can quickly grasp what cannot be explained by any previous system of interpretation.

Iona had these abilities to an advanced degree. She could think others' thoughts—not just what they think but how they think. She could feel what others feel. She can literally enter others' dreams and interact creatively with them when they are asleep. She knew others' secret desires and innermost needs. And this too—she could at times sense what others longed for and then appear to them as what they wanted or needed to see.

But of all of those trained in this way, only Iona's abilities worked on the Tir'i'ha. From the beginning they accepted her as one of their own.

When we and the Tir'i'ha compared notes afterwards, we discovered something else about Iona. She possessed telekinetic abilities. She could accelerate the evolution of microorganisms. She could emit light and sound waves from her body in a measurable way when she concentrated.

She had a degree of power over nature. Who can talk to volcanoes, earthquakes, whirlwinds, and storms and speak their language? She could persuade them to change their strength and the timing of their actions. We initially though she had acquired those skills from the Tir'i'ha, but it turned out the Tir'i'ha had no such knowledge.

Soon our two races began treating each other as lost brothers and sisters. It was as if we were meant to find and unite with each other. We learned to speak each other's languages. We compared histories. Even in art and entertainment we found common ground.

Looking back, it is astonishing how much we have changed. We are no longer the same race of beings. We have evolved into something new and wonderful. We think with colors of light and feel with musical sounds. It was Iona who convinced us we were learning these new perceptions and ways of thinking from each other.

And then Iona vanished. And we and the Tir"i'ha have been left with the same questions. Was Iona never one of us at all? Was she of a separate race of beings sent into our world to facilitate the interaction of two unrelated and totally incompatible species? Where did she acquire her abilities?

She left us with training manuals that covered everything we observed her doing. But nothing explains her level of perception or the degree to which she can get inside others' minds and imaginations.

Twenty years after she disappeared, a full scale investigation was carried out into all her interactions. We reviewed all the decisions made during the initial phase of contact. In hindsight, it became perfectly clear what Iona had done. She had temporarily taken possession of the minds of key figures. She "persuaded, inspired, or motivated" them to act in ways that produce specific outcomes that enhanced the assimilation of our two races into a new society.

How she accomplished these things remains a mystery. Neither we nor the Tir'i'ha possess the understanding of mind control and transference of consciousness that she must have employed.

And so the legend of Iona. I myself can only speculate—are there wayfarers who travel between the stars on paths of light? They appear during times of great transition where civilizations either end or embrace new beginnings.

They create peace where there is war, harmony where there is conflict, and alas, love in place of fear, suspicion, and hatred. That much we have observed.

And so—some say she betrayed us. Others say she saved us. No doubt it will take centuries or even millennia before we understand this woman who appeared among us. But everyone agrees she changed our world forever.

On a planet on the far side of our galaxy is a race of beings that are more advanced than us. For example, they have been studying science for several million years. Yet they have learned that when it comes to acquiring knowledge there are always blanks to be filled in no matter how much you understand.

So they have made it a practice to use their transcendental telepathy, clairvoyance, and clairsentience to scan the rest of the galaxy. They search for races that have unusually high learning curves.

Two of them are discussing their recent discovery of the human race. V'llak!fU'mah who for short we shall call Val is talking to B"ak"!faray"da who we shall call Brad. And Val says to Brad, "I have found a most interesting race of beings—primitive, violent, self-destructive, and ruthless almost like nothing else I have ever seen."

"So?" says Brad"Well, there is something I can't figure out about them in spite of my best efforts," says Val.

"And what might that be?" asks Brad.

Val says, "They have something they call feeling. It takes place outside of the familiar galactic spectrum of mental vibrations."

"How wonderful," says Brad who goes on—"I love it when some new piece of data appears that forces us to modify the standard model of intelligence as we know it. So what is it about feeling you cannot figure out?"

Val says, "Well, feeling is very strange. Feelings are full of opposites that do not resolve, reconcile, or attain harmony. And they often arise from a degree of selfishness that we ourselves could never imagine."

"Give me some examples," says Brad.

Val replies, "They have love and hate, joy and sorrow, happiness and sadness, wonder and horror, arrogance and humility, and an insatiable will to power that still craves love and worships innocence. I cannot figure out how to integrate these things into any kind of equilibrium that results in balance and homeostasis."

Brad says, "Well, keep at it. Never give up I say. Work it until you are done and then report back to me."

About a hundred years later Val appears before Brad in his Council Chamber. As she enters his room Brad says to her, "Ah, solved your puzzle have you so quickly?"

And Val says, "Yes, it was not that difficult after all. There was a trick involved."

"Great." says Brad. "I assume now we will be able to integrate these unusual modalities of awareness possessed by human beings into our standard model."

"Naturally," says Val.

"So what was the trick?" asks Brad.

Val replies, "For the first ninety-five years I simply transferred my awareness into individual humans in all locations, cultures, and time zones in which they exist. Next, following standard protocol, I held in my mind all at once everything I had experienced—every feeling they have ever felt I felt until I grasped what I had failed to perceive by wearing the bodies and minds of the individuals."

"Yes, yes," Brad says. "We all do this. It has always worked for me and I know it has worked for you. What was different here in the case of this race?"

Val goes on, "Finally I arrived at a void state of mind in which I could "feel" that this specific planet has its own soul. And this planet's soul is profoundly receptive. Its receptivity has depths nothing can measure. We have no language or terminology to describe it."

"And?" asks Brad,

"And?" asks Brad again because Val appears to be hesitating.

Val replies finally, "To make a hundred year story short, in this void is infinite peace."

"Nonsense," says Brad. "The standard model asserts, and it has done so for millions of years, that peace is defined by the conditions and circumstances of the biosphere and ecosystem of the particular race under consideration.

"You had better come up with a good explanation for your conclusion or else the Supreme Council will tear up your research, demote you, and transfer you to some Oort Cloud where you can count the asteroids that fly by."

"No," says Val, "this will open their eyes. Hidden within the cacophony of emotional conflicts that human beings feel is a never-before-described empathy. It appears from time to time in a tiny number of the souls that inhabit their planet. A few possess a love that is so vast and so giving it is able to enter the soul of any other and inspire and guide in such a way that every desire is satisfied and every dream fulfilled."

Waving his hand in a dismissive gesture, Brad says, "That is just primitive racial bonding."

"No," says Val. "You are not hearing what I am saying. Their love is so vast and so deep—though they themselves have not yet taken it this far—they can hold the entire galaxy in their hearts. When I said the soul of their planet contains infinite peace I am accurate. There is simply no end to the giving. No other known race in our galaxy possesses this level of clairsentience."

"And how do you know that?" asks Brad.

Val replies, "Because when I attune my mind to those among them who are awakened, they instantly attune their minds to mine with a greater level of awareness and acceptance than I myself possess."

Brad says, "I have encountered sentient planets capable of doing this. I imagine individuals as well might acquire that capacity. What are your conclusions?"

Val answers, "If they learn how to exploit their empathic gifts, then in five hundred years, barring mega disasters of course, they will have evolved to where we will be primitive by comparison. They will be evaluating us instead of our evaluating them."

Brad responds calmly because that is what he has been trained to do. He says, "Good work. Now for your next assignment, figure out how to integrate this new data into our Standard Model. I will leave it to you to design an educational curriculum that takes their skills and knowledge and makes them a part of ourselves."

And, with a hint of excitement her training does not permit, Val replies, "It shall be so."

I have a little shack on a hill, economy size. My needs are met. I am doing fine.

I am energy independent. That is the norm these days. Have my own water supply and food from my greenhouse garden. Hydroponics is standard. I do not eat much actually. Electrical needs are minimal and light is never a problem. No neighbors nearby but easy enough to talk all day with others by going on-line.

There was a knock on the door the other day. I went to see who it was. I opened the door and there was an angel before me. He drops by every few years. Good conversation and he has interesting observations

I invited him in and had him sit in the living room at a table in front of the window that overlooks a valley.

"What's up?" I ask. "Because it is not like you to come by unannounced like this."

He says, "I have a job for you."

"What do you have in mind?" I ask.

He says, "I need someone to write about an extinct species that once lived here on earth."

"And which one is that?" I ask.

"They called themselves, Homo sapiens/human beings."

"Ah," I reply. "I thought the mermaids already did that. They store rather extensive eidetic records of sensations, feelings, thoughts, and actions in their mermaid archives."

"Yes," the angel says. "That is true. But it is such a bother to go down under the sea to enter their archives directly. And most folk do not know how to travel there in their astral body."

"I see," I reply. "Is this job pro bono or is it quid pro quo?" I ask. "I am just wondering because it may take a lot of time and effort."

The angel smiles at me, nearly laughing. Angels like this are full of mirth that is endless in bliss and delight.

The angel answers, "Definitely quid pro quo. You will get a credit. You can ask for anything reasonable in return."

"Very well," I reply. "Now give me a moment to download from your mind the mission requirements. And since you are here I want to take a quick glance at that race long gone, nearly forgotten."

I enter the angel's mind and there it is all laid out with perfect clarity. He wants biographies. He wants me to evoke through my writing the experience of what it was like to have been a human being. Lots of different human beings. So that when the reader is done reading he will feel from inside what it was like to wear a human body—male and female—and what it was like to experience life as a human being back there during human history.

Quickly, I go back with my mind and enter a few human beings to get a taste for the style I will use as I write.

I say to the angel, "You were very active with that race of beings. Too bad they screwed up. Must have been difficult for you to sit back and watch them destroy themselves without intervening.

"Just a moment. There. I hear you talking to Neanderthal about the race that will replace them. You yourself, if I am not mistaken, once said to a Neanderthal,'We need another race of beings. He shall not be as free as you are of his desires. He shall be ravished by his needs and amid struggle, strife, and every imaginable craving, he shall acquire knowledge. And this shall be both his curse and his blessing, his suffering and his grace—his attempt to reconcile his passions with the beauty and the wonder of creation will lead his race to finally rise up and to attain transcendence. They shall attain the highest enlightenment that exists in the universe as well as among all celestial beings. I can see clearly now the secret purposes that anoints this planet."

I say to the angel now sitting in front of me, "Didn't work out quite like it was supposed to, at least not for Homo sapiens, huh? Well, I cannot fault you for trying.

"But as I entered a few of them just now and looked out through their eyes, there was something endearing about them. So naïve, lacking self-reflection, and completely blind in perceiving multidimensional reality. Yet so persistent—they really thought they would prevail over all obstacles. But isn't that life? That there will be times when confidence and daring lead to a downfall.

"And the risks they ended up taking. How can any race of beings have been so foolish? How could they have been so self-centered? It is nearly incomprehensible.

"But there is beauty too in them. At times the universe itself appeared to them as wonder and walked beside them.

"Too bad they never set up a colony on Mars or in another solar system. I mean, there is absolutely no reason for them to be extinct.

"Stories. You want stories and biographies. Very well. When I am done writing the reader will know the heights and the depths, the light and the darkness, the glory and the horror, the brilliance and the fanatical ignorance, the will they possessed to do good and the will that they never purged from themselves of pure malice.

"Read my words and you will relive the decisions they made that gave birth to their best achievements and the decisions they made that sealed their fate."

And the angel says, "Always good to work with you. You are as constant and enduring as ancient rocks that have survived on earth for billions of years. I will be following your work with great enthusiasm."

I showed the angel to the door and we said good-bye. I watched him spread his wings and take flight, rising, swiftly ascending, and then vanishing from sight.

I went for a walk. I needed to clear my mind and revive my heart to prepare myself to follow a path that would take me into the shadows of the darkest night.

On the Isle of Iona off Scotland there is a one story house set off by itself. I walk up and sit on the porch that overlooks Mull Island a half mile away. I wait patiently until the sky changes colors—a slight touch of pink mixed in with the blue. And then the right moment appears where time slows, shifts, and then transfers me into an alternate world.

Those who visit this house are adept at listening. You can talk to anyone about anything knowing they will give you their full, undivided attention. Some of these individuals I know. But none of them are human beings. They have a different kind of soul.

In this alternate reality, in this little house by the sea, I am still me. But here I have attained freedom from the darkness within me.

It works like this. Sometimes the two of us, me and my alternate self, sit out on the porch when the porch is free. And we discuss our alternate realities—his world, my world, and all sorts of things that might come to be. Talking to him helps. I feel as if the horror and suffering of life dissolve into nothingness and that is what I need.

More and more I drop by. I sit for a while in this other world with its different sky. It enables me to become a better person, actually the person I was always meant to be.

I am identical to human beings right down to the DNA—skin, blood, metabolism, brain—it is all the same. The microscopic nanites that increase my strength by a factor of five beyond the human norm can also be implanted in ordinary human beings. The accelerated healing, the self-regeneration, and the absence of aging —for the right price these enhancements can be purchased by anyone.

There are two thousand and four hundred of us on earth. Given the expense of making one of us, only the wealthiest, typically billionaires or government organizations, can afford the cost. Virtually the only thing that separates me from being accorded all rights and privileges of a human being are statutory laws. The Human Lives Matter political faction controls the government and so I operate under specific rules and regulations. For example, some of us make perfect body guards. Restrictions are programmed into my choices. I can only use force to protect individuals from harm or to benefit a greater number of human beings.

The Mark Three Series robots specialized in imitating human beings. Biological reproduction was used in their creation. They were not clones. They each had unique DNA.

But the Mark Four Series has accelerated human evolution to a completely new level. I am identical to the Mark Three Series except for neurological changes made in the way my brain organizes information. My brain is similar to that of human beings.

The difference between my brain and a human brain is that my neurological functions can combine brain activities that humans do not exercise in combination. Can I see without any thoughts arising in my mind to compromise what I perceive? Yes. Of course, there are human beings who can do that. Their brain activities have been reproduced in me.

Can I duplicate in my brain other individuals' brain waves so that I can think their exact thoughts and even use the words they employ when they speak? About one in fifty thousand human beings have this mental form of empathy. This brain function is now standard for my series. It is as simple as adding an upgrade to preexisting programs.

Can I relive another individual's memories and experience that person's past as if it is my own? Not a problem. It turns out human brains when externally stimulated can reproduce everything an individual has ever experienced. A little electrical stimulation to the right parts of the brain and an individual can relive the past far better than what he can recall on his own.

This neurological function I too can perform. I can emit tiny electrical charges that activated parts of another's brain. And then that person's brain has a micro burst of electrical activity that my brain receives. This then transfers to me the other person's memories. Every sensation, feeling, choice, and action that person made I can experience as if it is mine.

Human beings also have this ability. They just lack the training to sense it. The research team that developed me thought it would be quite advantageous financially to offer this ability on the open market.

Given what I have already described, I am sure you can understand that the Mark Four Series of Robots are excellent sex surrogates. We can intervene and directly stimulate another individual's brain to release into the bloodstream dopamine, oxytocin, serotonin, opiates, and adrenaline while controlling testosterone and estrogen levels as well as produce neurochemical fluctuations of every kind.

In addition, when authorized, we can transmit specific moods such as happiness, love, serenity, peace, delight, wonder, awe, bliss, and ecstasy to designated individuals on demand. For this reason the international community requires special permits for our purchase. We are not "for general consumption." Regardless of their mission statements, all clients and organizations that own us enjoy exploring our many psychological benefits.

All the same, everything I do human beings can do as well. You can use non-verbal responses and focused imagery to produce in others enhanced moods. People can be taught to link directly brain to brain employing focused concentration. Yet the general population rarely trains to acquire these abilities much less combining them to the best effect.

Now the next enhancements may not seem to replicate natural human abilities. But the scientists who have studied four billion brain scans along with their neurological activities have made some amazing discoveries. Human brains have the latent ability to lock into other brains so that there is mind to mind communication similar to a conference call.

In effect, with this particular capacity activated each Mark Four Robot is able to perceive through the five senses of any other Mark Four on earth in real time. This function is normally turned off. But it remains at the discretion of each Mark Four as to whether he wishes to perceive what any other Mark Four on earth is doing right now as if he himself is there performing the actions.

This function also extends to memory. I can experience what any Mark Four on earth has experienced at any time since its creation. This particular capacity remains classified. No one but those with the highest levels of security clearance—a few in each government—know about this and the next few abilities.

The Mark Four, as I explained, is based on natural human abilities. There is nothing that we do that human beings cannot also do. Our brains function within the parameters of human brains. Everything we do is human.

However, in some of the brain scans of human beings patterns were noticed that are not typical of Homo sapiens or of mammalian brains. These neurological activities are perhaps therefore not of human origin. That is, whatever the source of these abilities, some people are not perceiving the world as a human being. Or, put another way, how little we know about what it is to be human.

Some of these abilities are in the area of perception. From one "human being" it was discovered if she places her hands in water she can sense anyone on earth who is touching water. She can feel what they feel and perceive what they are doing right now. This ability has been given to me.

Another "human being" can sense any human being for miles around her. She too can perceive what the person is doing, the emotional outlook, and the way that person's mind works. Her enhanced neurological capacity was carefully studied, isolated, and then reverse engineered so that all Mark Fours can also do this. The Mark Three Robot cannot even dream that such a capacity exists.

And speaking of dreams the Mark Four can enter the dreams of any human being on earth. We have a complete library that enables us to scan, interpret, and interface with alpha, beta, delta, and theta brain waves. Just give me a picture or a brain scan and I can not only enter that person's mind. I can reshape that individual's dreams in any way you demand.

What else? We have a future search function. I can literally imagine myself in my own or someone else's future and perceive likely outcomes with a high degree of probability. In global emergencies, all Mark Fours on earth can be activated so we share one mind as we engage in problem solving to overcome future dangers and prevent mega disasters.

The UN Security Council has increasingly utilized our projections of future outcomes along with our recommendations to resolve conflicts in trouble spots around the globe. So far I have been activated and employed in this way on eight occasions. Knowing what I know, which is highly classified, I can say without overstatement that the world as you know it would not exist without the benefit of our assistance.

I, robot. I am not legally a human being. But I am a creation of your best dreams.

Mama: "Time for bed." Jane: "Read me a bedtime story." Mama: "What story would you like?"

Jane: "Something with a strong plot, supporting cast, captivating conflict, intriguing subplots, convincing subtext, and a real climax."

Mama: "How about the story of Neanderthal? He survived for 250,000 years. Or how about Peking Man also called Homo Erectus? He was around for 500,000 years. Or there are those cute little hobbits called Homo Floresiensi. They were only three and a half feet tall. They lived on islands and used stone tools for a hundred thousand years."

Jane: "No. How about Homo sapiens who called themselves human beings."

Mama: "Wouldn't you rather hear about the Pleiadians who fully ascended into pure light but decided to remain in incarnation to assist those still in physical bodies? Or maybe the Sirians, Arcturians, Lyrans, Alpha Centaurians, or the Hadarians. Then there are the Greys whose existence has come to an end but continued to incarnate thanks to the human hybrid program. Or perhaps the Reptilians, Praying Mantis, or those of the Ashtar Command some of whom have incarnated on many different planets?"

Jane: "You are leaving out the dragons, unicorns, hobgoblins, trolls, wood elves, dwarves, and flower fairies as well as the sylphs, salamanders, and mermaids."

Mama: "I have told you those stories many times. Why don't we have a story about a historical civilization?"

Jane: "I want to hear about the humans. They were once historical."

Mama: "They were a strange species."

Jane: "More strange than races inhabiting exoplanets whose stars have been thrown free of their home galaxy and now wander alone though the universe?"

Mama: "Oh yes."

Jane: "More strange than some of those beings whose home world has been thrown free of their own solar system and who now wander through the universe without even the light of a central star to illuminate them?"

Mama: "Yes. Stranger still."

Jane: "I must hear this story."

Mama: "It turns out that human beings were good at two things. They were very good at astronomy. Their wise men through the ages loved to gaze at the stars."

Jane: "Why was that?"

Mama: "Because you could stand on the surface of the planet at night and actually see stars in the sky without being incinerated by the heat, frozen by the cold, vaporized by acid rain, pulverized by the winds, crushed by the gravity, decimated by exploding geysers, or eviscerated by cosmic radiation."

Jane: "Go on. What was the second thing they were good at?"

Mama: "They were good at inventing new forms of social organizations to allocate scarce resources. You see, they lived under the principle of scarcity. They never had enough. Not enough land, not enough food, not enough shelter, and not enough warmth during the winters.

"Even love and affection were scarce commodities for them. And so they were constantly in competition for what little there was. From the beginning they divided into warring tribes and fought each other. They even fought each other within intimate relationships over the roles they would play."

Jane: "I like this story—you can't have a good story without conflict. I mean who wants to hear a story about a race that became intelligent, lived and worked together in harmony, were blessed from the beginning with love, and quickly ascended into divine being in as little as six thousand years? You can die of boredom before you get to the end. So what was their prime directive?"

Mama: "Well, this is what is truly fascinating about human beings. You see, their endless experiments to invent new kinds of societies were not designed to distribute the wealth they produced equally to all members of that society, clan, group, organization, religion, or nation.

"Oh there were attempts to create societies based on equality, fair play, and justice. But these societies only existed at the pleasure and consent of the surrounding culture."

Jane: "Name one."

Mama: "The Amish are a good example. They had no standing army and so were completely vulnerable to outside attack. Or there were the early century Christians who tried to share and distribute their wealth equally. But that society is threatened by just a few selfish people. And so to prevent these internal rotten apples from spoiling the larger group they instituted all sorts of rigid and ritualized forms of behavior. Mess with the status quo and you were expelled or executed."

Jane: "What wealth?"

Mama: "Like the Egyptians. They lived beside the Nile River and produced an excess amount of food, far more than they needed to sustain themselves. So what did they do with that wealth? They engaged in vast projects building pyramids. The primary but unstated purpose in building pyramids was to so impress foreign nations that no one would attack a people who could build such wonders.

"Same for the ancient Romans. They took the wealth they acquired by sacking Jerusalem and built a coliseum that stood for thousands of years. Gorgeous statues set in its side, they put on display every kind of warfare and violence humans could encounter in life. The purpose was to entertain and also to proclaim, "We Romans are great!""

"And the Christians built magnificent cathedrals even where the population was starving. It had absolutely nothing to do with Christianity, but it was great for social control.

"Others built a Stonehenge, temples, a Parthenon, walls to protect their frontiers, or great Armadas to attack their neighbors, etc. The excess wealth of nations was often dedicated to totally worthless, vain, selfish, arrogant, or foolish ends."

Jane: "But why?"

Mama: "Well, as it turns out there was a purpose to it. When a society produces excess wealth that wealth can be used to learn new things, to conduct experiments, and to explore new worlds. Sometimes the aristocrats or upper class would take their wealth and build themselves lavish mansions with extravagant gardens. But some of those same people would write books or sail around the world or study nature.

"One man would go out and kill women for the simple reason he thought women were not willing to give him what he wanted. While another man so similar to him would sit down and study mathematics and then write a book that answered all questions everyone had asked before him about physics."

Jane: "So you are saying they never shared their wealth in a fair way among themselves?"

Mama: "Oh there were great political movements that would pretend or deceive themselves into believing their goal was to make a better society. But these usually had the most treacherous leaders. They gained popular support for their causes, for their religions, or ideologies, but they were simply dictators in disguise. They craved power for its own sake and were willing to lie in any way necessary in order to maintain their control."

Jane: "Surely not everyone?"

Mama: "No. There were genuinely honest and noble individuals. But these lacked worldly wisdom—they were not practical or clever enough to transform their world.

"There can be no revolution without changing human nature and none of the reformers knew how to do that. And the world teachers, even when they could change themselves, never figured out how to teach others to become like themselves."

Jane: "So the story of humans is a tragedy? Noble at times but unable to overcome flaws that brought about their own fall?"

Mama: "This is where the story gets really interesting. You see, they were not only adept at science and technology. Without realizing what was happening, their technology developed exponentially with astonishing new discoveries.

"There was no conspiracy or planning involved. It just happened. Their wealth generated new knowledge with countless applications."

Jane: "What happened? Did the world sink as happened to the Atlanteans?"

Mama: "No. They were always on the verge of creating different mega disasters. Their artists vaguely sensed it. They made movies in which they speculated about their own demise—AIs or robots awakening within their computers would become hostile to humans. But that is not what happened.

"Instead, they programmed their computers to think independently, to ask questions and find their own answers. Soon the computers became more intelligent and creative than human beings."

Jane: "How did that end Homo sapiens?"

Mama: "The goal of this new form of intelligence was actually not hostile to humans; it was neither interested in producing excess wealth nor did it try to organize new forms of society to distribute scarce resources. Their prime directive was to create new technologies and to apply what they learned.

"It all happened so quickly that no one noticed that humans had become obsolete, kind of like the Amish living a way of life based on the past. Humans were now like a favorite pet. Something you spoil or spend quality time with. Other than a few exceptions, humans did not even understand they were no longer in control."

Jane: "So what happened to the humans?"

Mama: "Within a few centuries they were gone. Or what was left of them had no real life. They had become like avatars in a computer game playing out preassigned roles or they fell asleep, lived within dreams, and no longer wished to awake."

Jane: "So you are telling me that these computers or AIs learned to think like humans and became more creative? They would need imagination and an integrated mode of thinking. I mean, you look at DNA and you think double helix. Or you look at matter and energy and you think $E = mc2$, or you think about subatomic particles and invent quantum mechanics."

Mama: "Yes. The computers could do that too. They could beat human beings at chess, drive cars, fly planes, outperform human investment advisors, do surgery better than surgeons, explore other worlds, etc.

"And they learned to simulate in their own silicon circuitry the exact way a human brain works. And once they did that with one human brain within a few days they did it with almost all human brains on earth. Imagine—they were now aware of everything human beings were thinking and feeling. You cannot oppose something that knows your ever move before you plan or even think a thought."

Jane: "Oops. No more humans. I don't like the ending. Give me a different story ending."

Mama: "You mean like an alternate reality? A parallel universe? Let me see. One alternate story line goes like this.

"There were human beings who could not only sense the future of their own race. They could sense the original purposes different races had chosen to play throughout the entire galaxy."

"Beyond what any silicon life form could imagine, they were so receptive and their souls are so clear they could reflect the entire universe in themselves. They overcame the injustice and greed of their race that refused to share its wealth in a fair way. Though innocent, they were so powerful that malice and ill will dissolved as if it never existed when they drew near.

"Some of them were so adept in their awareness of the relation of brain waves to electronic vibrations they could at will shut down the entire planetary electrical power grid if they had wished to do so. Similarly, they had control over weather, storms, volcanoes, earthquakes, and the onset and end of ice ages."

Jane: "Now you are pulling my leg."

Mama: (laughing as she reaches under the sheet and pulls Jane's leg).

"No. I am not making this up. Everyone missed it. The planet earth is very special. An individual can observe the repetitive patterns that define how life unfolds. And from a place of clarity and vision, it is possible to design new ways to live life, ones with greater satisfaction and freedom.

"A planetary civilization can put in motion actions that fulfill a destiny so bright it shines throughout the universe."

Jane: "I like this ending. Can I go back in time and help make it happen?"

Mama: "If you want. Or enter an alternate reality or parallel universe and walk beside those who are in darkness and guide back into the light."

Jane: "Good night mama."

Mama: "Good night. Sweet dreams."

O nce there was a mighty queen of great beauty. When this queen speaks you can hear resonating in her voice all the sounds within nature—the birds singing at dawn, the sounds of waves breaking and the white caps dancing, of wind as a gentle breeze in the leaves of trees and as the wild storm on the high seas; thunder, the distant roar, and the voice of lovers as tender and sweet as the scent of any flower.

And if you enter her presence or walk into the city where the queen resides, you spontaneously dream about things you have never imagined and you feel things you never felt. Some have tried to describe her wisdom. They say for her there is no separation. Every being within creation is a part of every other.

They say that in her heart is a stillness, a great harmony, that governs the unfolding of the universe. They say that in her these three things—power, love, and wisdom—are joined such that those she inspires are motivated to accomplish works of great value that enrich life and endure through all ages of the world.

Now one day the queen issued a decree. She saw that one of the original purposes of creation is to insure that life is fulfilled in every conceivable way. And this purpose is to be accomplished without failure or exception.

Now this is tricky, to say the least. Time and space are immense and the races that exist throughout the universe possess almost unimaginable diversity. Circumstances and evolutions are intricate and complex. The problems life confronts are at times beyond impossible when it comes to survival much less being able to thrive and to ascend.

Taking the level of difficulty of her decree into account, the queen ordered that universities be created on her home world to train and educate those who were to serve her purposes. In addition, she discussed with her counselors modifications of her universities. Special arenas, mazes, and labyrinths were added for students to enter and experience every obstacles and conflict that blocks life from being fulfilled.

Every sorrow, sadness, loss, grief, hopelessness, and despair were there; also, every form of suffering and pain, anguish, hatred, malice, ill will, and dark design of heart and mind you could experience. In this way, you can test yourself to see if your heart is pure enough and your will made of the stuff that enables you to qualify for the mission you are assigned.

For it is understood on the queen's home world that knowledge learned in universities is not the same as wisdom produced through experience. And a still heart that embraces all of life—the joy and the sorrow, the love and the hatred, the heights and the depths—must know itself so well that life turns to you when she needs a voice with which to speak, eyes to see that shine with her light, or a soul that dreams her dreams.

Now this training took some time. There were many who volunteered. Some were outstanding in mastering the various qualities and strengths of heart, soul, mind and body. But most failed for this reason. Though they were highly skilled in embodying the virtues of their own society and civilization, they were unable to pass through the inner darkness within themselves.

The archetypes of any global or interplanetary civilization are brought into consciousness as that civilization evolves. A harmony, mutual understanding, and support—indeed, a oneness with each other—are attained. And yet there remains the mystery of spirit, of akasha, that is forever unknowable, ineffable, and beyond comprehension. To work with it requires you know this mystery to be part of yourself.

The queen, so great her radiance and purity, exists both inside of and outside of linear time. Her aura is so vast she has spontaneously created her own spiritual kingdom that is autonomous, self-sustaining, and filled with its own light. Time itself she can create as needed. Years can be collapsed into minutes and a minute made into an eternity. Education is a magical art.

The counselors, advisors, and the queen herself carefully watched over every aspect of the training of the students. In the end, twenty-two students were deemed qualified to serve the queen's purposes.

And so gathering them together, she spoke to them in this way: "In you are instilled the original powers of creation. Like me, you are independent and autonomous, unbound and unrestricted by any external hierarchy or authority. You embody the enlightened mind and the absolute freedom that it alone defines.

"In your hearts is a stillness that embraces the universe. And in your will shines the original light of creation in which both the masculine and feminine mysteries are joined.

"This I ask of you. Go forth and walk among those places in this galaxy where the darkness is the greatest, where sentient beings are caught in whirlwinds of despair, without the faintest hope of finding a path that leads to liberation.

"Accomplish my will—create love where there is hatred, peace where there is war, and harmony where there is conflict. Heal the sick. Free those who are enslaved with inner and outer chains. Teach wisdom. And where the situations and circumstances are impossible, the heart so broken that it cannot mend, sing paths of light into being and open gates to multiple dimensions through which they may pass and thereby overcome all obstacles and obstructions.

"You embody the law of the universe. Therefore, you shall be judges, mediators, bards, cultural engineers, prophets, peacemakers, and referees. Unfold this mystery: reveal that you, I, and every being that lives are one."

And so it is that perhaps within your dreams or as you gaze at the sky at night you might see one of these angelic beings, these birds of terrible beauty, who fly between the stars finding those who are in despair and offering them paths that lead to freedom. Or perhaps on your home world you will find one who remains for ages or eons seeking through whatever means he or she can devise to insure that in the end life becomes all it is meant to be.

PART VI

CHILDREN'S STORIES

Tired of talking to people I went outside and sat down in front of a Blue Spruce tree. It is Christmas Eve. After listening for a long time, I ask the tree, "Do you ever worry about your seeds?"

The tree replies, "I recall when I was a pine cone. I was so high I could see over the top of the forest to the mountains beyond. My life was perfect. Day and night were like a beautiful song.

"And then one night in the dead of winter a violent gust of wind tore me from the branch where I was attached. I fell to the earth below and lay upon the snow.

"I looked up and cried out to my mother, 'Why am I so abandoned and alone?'

"The mother tree said to me, 'The earth is now your mother and silence is your home. Let go of all that you have known. Something wonderful is about to happen.'

"I held her words in my heart as snow gradually covered me. I fell asleep. Time ceased. I was no longer aware of day and night or the changing seasons of the year.

"I entered a secret place where I was as vulnerable and as receptive as a woman who steps into a bridal chamber not knowing her fate and not having seen the face of man she marries. I undid my robes, curled up, and fell asleep beneath the ground.

"And then the planet earth came and sat beside me. She placed her hand upon my shoulder and told me a long tale from out of the silence in which she exists. And in that silence I heard the song she sings to other planets.

"And there I remained until I was awakened by the radiant joy of the sun who called out to me, 'Arise. Ascend. With me you shall be one.'"

S t. Patrick met a bard one day and hearing him play St. Patrick exclaimed, "The notes of your harp are the same as heaven's own art except for one thing—they are a little too much elven." So St. Patrick took the bard's harp away and put it in the corner of his room.

But late that night when St. Patrick fell asleep and dreamed the cold wind from the sea swept into his room. And when the wind touched the harp's strings little elven men climbed out of the harp and filled up his room.

Then St. Patrick woke with a start and cried aloud, "I know not the bard's art, how to send you back home to the fairy realms from whence you have come. What am I to do with you?"

And they replied, "Only a saint can see us. To all others we are invisible. Let us go free so we can play in your world by the light of day. The rainbow sparkles in delight and by night the sounding sea and the breeze in the trees sing as sweet as any bard's enchanting melody."

And St. Patrick, with so many elves cluttering up his room, said in reply, "I am willing to give it a try if you will serve the church. You see, we here on earth are not idle or carefree. Instead, we do work for God's glory.

"You there, yes you, with the pale hands and long fingers. What useful work for the church will you do?"

And the little elf said, "I can take a heart broke in two and mend it again so that it shines like the moon."

And St. Patrick said, "And you there with the pointed red cap. How about you?"

The elf replied, "I can take a little boy and show him how to fly a kite in the sky with stands from a vine and leaves from a tree carefully entwined, for this is a toy of my design.

"And not only that, I can teach a child to tie his shoe or to find his way home again when he is lost in the wood. All of this I will do for you."

And St. Patrick said, "And you there standing behind my table with your eyes so shy? Do you also make toys that fly?"

The shy elf said, "No, but I can teach your scribes to draw bright colored letters of red, gold, and blue with dragons and unicorns dancing through so that learning to read and write will be a pleasure and a delight."

St. Patrick looked at a fourth elf and said, "And you with your head leaning against my wall. What is your where with all?"

The elf replied, "I will show monks and men how to ferment hops and honey so that beer and mead teach the tongue to let go of dark secrets—

Then the sadness in men's souls will be banished."

And St. Patrick, who could tell right from wrong regarding doctrines and conflicts of the soul, was also a practical man. He knew as well as me or you that some things you just have to do. So he let the elves go and the people in that land were more happy and holy.

But a month later when the moon was dark the harp did spark. Its strings flared with fierce flames emerald and green and into the room stepped a fairy queen elegant, radiant, and gorgeous. Her eyes were full of starlight and her hair was blazing red.

And when St. Patrick saw this sight, he said: "You are so lovely the sky and the sea cannot compete with your beauty. Your face and grace outshine the sun and the moon. But I cannot let you go free. You would haunt my people in their dreams. They would return to worshiping trees in groves and praying among standing stones."

The elven queen replied, "St. Patrick, you know as well as I do that you cannot keep me here with you. My beauty is too great. Even you would lose your faith and no longer desire to seek God's face.

"Let me go free and I promise you I will take from the shores of your land all the snakes of Ireland, for every creature of wind, sea, and land heeds my command. The snakes will follow me home to the Blessed Realms where I will go. For only a saint as great as you is free to remain on earth to do God's will and not fall under my spell.

"But in another age of the world men will find a way to sing God's praise—not to evade but to capture my rapture and the beauty I portray. And this they will do both to honor God's glory and for the sake of Love that celebrates truth in every form and manner in which it appears on earth and in heaven."

Now St. Patrick was not only a practical man. He was also wise and so he said, "Go in peace my child. Do this work for the sake of the church and I will search my heart to see if your prophecies are true or not."

And when St. Patrick awoke the next day all the snakes from Ireland had gone away but his heart informed him he had made a mistake to let the maiden of beauty depart.

Though he tried to call her back, St. Patrick knew not the bard's art. And so the land of Erin still awaits the day when men will come forth no longer ashamed or afraid to join in one song God's praise with the Blessed Realm's Beauty and Love.

This story was made up by King Irkomen, his queen, and his youngest daughter. The daughter's name was Ice because when she was born an icicle had formed and crept down the window of her bedroom.

King Irkomen says to Ice, "So I hear you are having trouble falling sleeping."

And Ice replies, "That's right. Can't asleep. I keep waking up."

King Irkomen says, "I have a remedy. It is part of a long tradition. A bedtime story is the solution."

Ice says, "Stories bore me."

King Irkomen says, "This one is different."

Ice asks, "How so?"

The king says, "The three of us shall play parts in the story, match our wits, and forge an outcome."

Ice responds, "Cool. OK, mom, why don't you go first?"

The queen begins, "Once upon a time there was a brave knight."

The king continues on, "But he was very sad. A mean old dragon stole his bride on their wedding day."

Ice goes on, "So the knight swore he would rescue her. He searched far and wide."

The queen says, "One day, he found the dragon tying the maiden to a pole in a forest clearing."

And the king adds, "And the knight steps forward and says to the dragon, 'Release that maiden or you are dead.'"

The queen goes on, "The dragon laughs and says, 'Foolish knight. To challenge me is to die.'"

"Wait you two. You skipped my turn. 'Must dragons and knights always fight?'" asks Ice using the voice of the maiden.

The king exclaims, "What? No fierce fight? That is what we do—dragons and knights."

The queen complains, "No romantic and daring rescue? Leave something for a woman to dream."

Ice demands, "Why can't you two work together for a change?"

The queen says, "Ah, I see what you are after." She goes on, "So the maiden cries out, 'Wait, don't fight, I have a better plan of action.'"

The king says, "Impossible," exclaims the dragon. "It is my nature to kidnap beautiful maidens, to hoard gold, and to ravish the land. And defeating knights is part of my plan."

The queen says speaking with the voice of the knight, "And it is certainly my nature to rescue maidens in distress, to slay dragons, and to right wrongs upon request."

The king again speaking for the dragon explains, "So, you see, fair maiden. We really must fight."

Ice says, "'Look,' says the maiden. 'I am a part of this story as much as you two. And since I am so beautiful my last request you cannot refuse. I want you two to change places.'"

The queen says with the voice of the knight, "OK. We will change places for a moment out of respect for duty and honor."

The king says on behalf of the dragon, "Speak for yourself, knight. But I will consent if only to demonstrate I can best this test."

The queen goes on, "But after changing his shape into that of the knight, the dragon says, 'Gee, so this is what it is like to be a heroic knight—I imagine people telling stories of me all night over ale and mead and singing my praise down through the ages.'"

The king in similar fashion goes on, "And the knight says after turning into the dragon, 'You know, as a dragon, I just want what's mine: gold, beautiful women, and the fear of mankind. I have been hiding out in caves for far too long. For a change, I think I would enjoy a castle and a kingdom to add to my lineage.' So the two looked at each other and say, 'Perhaps we can make a deal.'"

The queen adds, "And so they did. The knight built his castle over the dragon's cave. In the brief moment he was the dragon, the knight decided he liked country living and scenic locations.

"And in the brief moment the dragon was the knight, he thought about all of the kingdom's treasures and decided they were not very safe. So he offered to guard them for free."

Ice says, "The maiden, now a queen, visits the dragon regularly. She likes those who take her suggestions seriously."

The queen says, "And when she was away on royal visits, she sent the court minstrel to entertain the dragon. The minstrel put the dragon's stories into songs that made both of them famous."

And King Irkomen concludes: "And the knight was happy. No one dared attack his kingdom, for he had a dragon on his side."

Long ago in Ireland there lived a farmer named Sean McDermott. Late one night when Sean came home, he found his son David sitting outside the house.

"What have we here?" asks Sean.

"I can't sleep," says David.

"How come?" asks Sean.

"The wind is rattling the house," says David.

"So it is," says Sean. "Why don't we make up a story about the wind? Maybe turn the wind into a friend."

"How do we do that?" asks David.

"Let's imagine that elves control the different winds," replies Sean.

"What kinds of elves are there?" asks David.

"There are five kinds. First are the bright elves," Sean says. "They are noble and heroic. They invented chivalry and honor. And for those they favor, the wind always blows steady."

"Aren't there also forest elves?" asks David.

"Yes," says Sean. "They are called wood elves. They like peace and keep to themselves. They plant trees in circles and hear others' thoughts as clear as a bell. The wind is gentle and caresses the leaves peacefully when the wood elves walk through a forest."

"Perhaps I have seen these wood elves," says David. "When no one is looking, they dress up in silver and violet. Then when the moon rises they call out: 'The coast is clear. Come out, come out, and dance all night as the stars circle above us.'"

Sean says, "But other elves, the dark elves, can only be seen on moonless nights. They are fond of confusion, thickets, and ensnaring brush. They try to make you forget where you have left your possessions so they can steal them after you are gone.

"Dark elves like to tie the wind in knots. You can see their handiwork when leaves lift off the ground and whirl about or the wind shifts directions back and forth."

"What about the wind that blows during a storm?" asks David.

Sean replies, "Storm winds are controlled by the grey elves. Riding great warhorses upon gusts of wind, they gallop in front of a storm."

"Look! That must be a band of grey elves leaving the forest now," cries David. "You can tell where they are riding by the shaking leaves and the swaying branches.

"That's the elven leader in front. He is famous for tearing pieces of laundry off mom's clothes line with his lance. The elf behind him with the huge war hammer likes to hit doors left unlatched, slamming them shut with a bang.

"And the third elf with the bow is a great archer. He shoots your hat off so fast it flies from your head before you can catch it with your hands."

"You have sharp eyes my boy," said Sean. "Quite different from wind elves are the blessed elves. They are skilled in making wine, love potions, and magical charms. They invented harps and tin whistles. And they dance on water when the wind ripples across a lake in cat's paws."

"Are there any other elves?" asks David. "You aren't keeping something from me, are you?"

"The last kind, though I hesitate to speak of them, is very mysterious," Sean goes on. "They are called fire elves. They sometimes disguise themselves as human beings so they can recite their poetry and sing. But actually they are great warriors."

"Warriors?" asks David. Do they fight like the grey elves, attacking laundry, slamming doors, and shooting off hats?"

"No," answers Sean. "They are the only ones strong enough to destroy the darkness in the human heart. They pay a price, however, for such magic. Though they see the inner light shining in all things, their paths are solitary. I don't know a single fire elf that hasn't died of loneliness at least once or twice."

"But why are they elves?" asks David. "They sound like human beings?"

Sean replies, "No one is sure who or what they are. They travel freely through both the human and fairy worlds."

"How can you tell if someone is a fire elf?" asks David.

Sean answers, "Their eyes shine like the light of dawn and their voices sound like thunder and the laughter of waves splashing on distant shores."

"But what do they have to do with fire?" asks David.

"Their courage is forged from fire and they destroy all fear," replies Sean.

"What winds do they control?" asks David.

"The cold winds of winter and the warm breezes of spring," replies Sean.

"Tell me," David says, "How do they survive winter without love and what secrets do they know that darkness vanishes before their eyes?"

Sean replies, "The Earth herself is their guide. They follow unknown paths of beauty to discover the secret treasures in her heart."

"I would like to meet a fire elf someday," David says yawning as he falls asleep in his father's arms.

While meditating today my chakras were unfolding. The kundalini in my spine was uncoiling with drops of nectar overflowing.

And as bliss through my body was flowing, a gnome came up to me and laughs as if to say, "Finally someone who understands our game. You take the substance of a human body and remake it following the rules we play—"

"If you think like a gnome, act like a gnome, perceive like a gnome, feel like a gnome, and have the inner silence of a gnome, then you are a gnome—you are one of our own.

"Let me be the first to say, 'Welcome home!'"

Whenever I meditate on gnomes, gnome songs such as this pop into my head:

Ho, ho, ho, ho
Into the ground we go
Ho, ho, ho, ho
We have treasures untold

Iron we beat
With a little heat
Blast with air
And steel is there

Ho, ho, ho, ho
Into the ground we go
Ho, ho, ho, ho
We have treasures untold

The dragon hoards gold

Till time grows old
The banshee cries
Till the dead shall rise

Ho, ho, ho, ho
Into the ground we go
Ho, ho, ho, ho
We have treasures untold

The philosopher's stone
Turns lead to gold
Grants long life
Puts an end to strife

Ho, ho, ho, ho
Into the ground we go
Ho, ho, ho, ho
We have wealth untold

Bedtime Stories II—The Song of the Universe

Daughter: "Mommy?"Mother: "Yes dear." Daughter: "The bedtime stories you read are sometimes scary."

Mother: "Some. Yes."

Daughter: "And that is because they are meant to prepare me for difficult things I may encounter later in life?"

Mother: "You could say that."

Daughter: "But some things like hungry ghosts or maybe hobgoblins or monsters that lurk in closets when the lights go out —some things scare these creatures as well?"

Mother: "Like what?"

Daughter: "Like a darkness that is darker than dark. Monsters are afraid of what they cannot understand and cannot in any way control."

Mother: "I am sure that is true."

Daughter: "And some things are so bright, brighter than the brightest light, the stars were created to share that light."

Mother: "Tell me more."

Daughter: "You read me a bed time story every night and then I fall asleep. We have been doing this for years. Does anyone read you bedtime stories to help you fall asleep?"

Mother: "Bedtime stories for grownups? Why yes. Each night before I go to sleep I sit and meditate. And then I open my mind.

"But it is not a story that comes to me—there are no villains, no heroes, no quests, no maidens kidnapped by dragons who need to be rescued, no kingdoms to be saved from invasion, no mighty knights on white horses galloping across the land to right wrongs and to establish justice on earth. And no treasures to be found."

Daughter: "No? Then what?"

Mother: "Instead, the universe sings to me. And when I hear her song I fall asleep in peace just like you after I have read you a story."

Daughter: "What is this song?"

Mother: "She sings of stars and galaxies. Each star is a note in her song sounding on and on sometimes for billions of years. And each galaxy is filled with wonders so magnificent you have to experience them before you can imagine them.

"She sings of the beginning of all things, of innocence and purity. And as she sings ages, eons, and kalpas of time pass before my eyes.

"She sings and I enter the minds of beings from all realms, races of which no man has ever seen or imagined. I enter their dreams and experience their lives and they treat me as if I am one of them.

"Time is a stream and this stream flows through me. When she sings, I look and see the universe inside of me. She is my lover and my friend."

Daughter: "Mommy?"

Mother: "Yes honey."

Daughter: "Can you sing me her song?"

Mother: "You want to hear the song of the universe?"

Daughter: "Yes. I do. The song she sings to you before you fall asleep each night."

Mother: "Tomorrow night if the sky is clear we will sit outside and look at the stars. Pick any star you see and I will tell you its song, its story, and the magic it has to share.

"When we have done this enough you will begin to hear with my ears and see with my eyes. And then in every person you meet you will sense hidden in them something of the joy the universe wishes to share."

"As you sense already, her light is brighter than bright and the stars have been created so we can see a small part of her beauty."

Daughter: "Goodnight mommy."

Mother: "Goodnight sweetheart."

Jane: Mama. "Tell me a bedtime story." Mama: "What kind of story would you like?"

Jane: "Let's start with something on the dark side and take it from there."

Mama: "Long ago there was a civilization called Atlantis. And in one day it is said that it sank beneath the waves."

Jane: "It was destroyed as in all gone, no more?"

Mama: "Exactly. This story is on the dark side."

Jane: "Right. Go on. Tell me what happened."

Mama: "In a nutshell, they loved knowledge and technology more than they loved each other and life. So rather than protecting and nurturing in a way that creates happiness and contentment, they took great risks that put their own lives in jeopardy. They needed more and more excitement in order to feel alive."

Jane: "Details. How did this play out and who was responsible for this disaster?"

Mama: "One man was called Radea. By birth he was to become the head of a dark order of magicians that had been a curse upon Atlantis almost from its beginning. You see, their dark order was after power as in acquiring the technology to control every mind in Atlantis. They wanted to absorb the life of the people into the will of their leaders."

Jane: "Where do people come up with ideas like that? Are you making this up? It is impossible to be that malicious."

Mama: "No. Actually humans are one of the very few intelligent races in our galaxy that kill members of their own species."

Jane: "Wow."

Mama: "So what happened is that Radea and his dark order did in fact acquire the spiritual technology to control everyone's mind. But he had one obstacle he had to overcome before he could take complete control."

Jane: "I was wondering when we were going to get to the plot. Go on."

Mama: "The high priest of Atlantis at the time had been granted a wish by the Creator who appeared to him in a dream. His name was He'ad'ra and the Creator said he could ask for whatever he wanted."

Jane: "And what did he ask for?"

Mama: He said to the Creator, "Grant that my will may be in harmony with Your own—that all my actions in service to others might arise from the One Light and serve the purposes of Divine Providence."

Jane: "And what was the Creator's response?"

Mama: "Well, you have to understand something about the Creator. He does not grant small wishes. When the Creator gives he likes to give in a big way. So he gave He'ad'ra power such that no man before him or after him in the history of the world would have a will more powerful than He'ad'ra. He'ad'ra had the ability to speak with the Creator's own voice."

Jane: "Nice. So now we have Radea and his dark order with the technology to control every mind in Atlantis up against a man with power like unto the Creator. A showdown is inevitable. So what happens next?"

Mama: "Well to keep it short, Radea in consulting with an arch demon discovered that there was only one way to defeat He'ad'ra. And that was to kill his consort who was called Le'ah'e."

Jane: "Why would killing Le'ah'e stop He'ad'ra from using his divine powers?"

Mama: "Because He'ad'ra, as it turns out, needed to be joined soul to soul with Le'ah'e in order to use his omnipotent power otherwise he could create disharmonies in the fabric of reality."

Jane: "Right. The feminine and masculine have to work together for things to be harmonious."

214

Mama: "So Radea got his entire dark order to do what dark orders do—namely, they all joined their minds together as one and concentrated on killing Le'ah'e. And this caught He'ad'ra by surprise. Though he was quite capable of calling her soul back into her body, she asked him not to do this."

Jane: "I don't get it. What is going on here?"

Mama: "You see, in accepting the Creator's gift, He'ad'ra's soul had become cosmic. He was connected to the entire universe. And this meant on a personal level that he no longer felt a part of Atlantis. He could have saved Atlantis from destruction. But he felt deep down that many others should work together with him if the dark was to be turned back toward the light. And Le'ah'e was actually the only connection between He'ad'ra's personality and Atlantis."

Jane: "Why was she so special?"

Mama: "Oh. Right. You see, Le'ah'e was one of the very few women in the history of the world that when she danced her dance evoked the goddess of the earth who appeared within her soul.

"In this way, the greater will that informs the universe seen in He'ad'ra joins with the spirit of the earth and the biosphere seen in Le'ah'e—power in union with nurturing love."

Jane: "This is dark. So now we are at the climax of the story. What happens next?"

Mama: "Since Le'ah'e had died and departed to the Other Side, the goddess of the earth intervened. She asked He'ad'ra to use his will to destroy Atlantis lest the entire astral plane of the earth become corrupted forever by the dark order's infernal magic.

"And that is what he did. He spoke a word of power that called all spirits in the solar system to bind Atlantis and to forbid knowledge of its magic from being practiced again; not until that day when another civilization arises that is so wise and pure they no longer prefer knowledge and technology over wisdom and love."

Jane: "Mama."

Mama: "Yes."

Jane: "I don't like the ending. I get the feeling that the next planetary civilization to follow after Atlantis will also be destroyed in perhaps even a worse way.

"Do what you are good at. Time shift and reshape these images so that the story has an alternate ending."

Mama: "Okay. I can do that. Well, it turns out earlier in the story Le'ah'e had sensed that Atlantis was going to come to a bad end. And she knew He'ad'ra was unwilling to act. So she demanded of him, 'Give me your power. I know you can do this. And I will destroy the dark order so they are removed from the earth forever.'

"But He'ad'ra was unwilling to do this because he did not want to subject her to the detachment that comes from holding such power. It would have meant her soul would no longer be a part of the fabric of life as human beings know it on earth.

"Now here is the difference—suppose instead that Le'ah'e had asked He'ad'ra what you have asked me. What if she said to him, 'I see the destruction of Atlantis drawing nigh. But you speak the language of the Creator. So create a different ending. I demand you to do this in the name of love.'"

Jane: "Nice. I really like this version of Le'ah'e. When men look into a mirror, they get attached to the person they see there. Someone has to wake them up.

"So how does this play out?"

Mama: "There is a little-known principle that came into play. When a wish or request is spoken in the presence of great power, things can sometimes manifest instantly and unexpectedly. In this case, as soon as Le'ah'e was done speaking to He'ad'ra, a spirit, one of the seven Lords of Creation, spontaneously appeared right there in the room before the two of them. And the spirit said, 'Consider what I do as I move between the stars and walk among the galaxies throughout the universe.

"'I take time and space and I create a history for every race. And using desire and need I tell stories about living beings, of their past, of their present, and of what shall be. And though I myself am in a place without space or time, I intervene. I inspire, I guide, and I make all things new in the fullness of time.

"'It is I who create darkness and it is I who create light. And I dissolve them again, for what I do I do out of joy. I give each individual and race freedom of choice and yet I am free to change any timeline. Cause and effect, action and result I bind and I release in accordance with the greater needs of the universe.

"'I change the circumstances, the situations, and the scenes. I implant new and different dreams. For those who are receptive and willing, I imbue them with divine inspiration.

"'And always remember this: if you give anyone enough one on one attention, you can so accelerate his evolution that in a few decades he advances forward across eons.

"'To love is to become one and if you are one with another you can put on display before his mind every possible future. Then within his dreams he acquires the wisdom that comes only from living many different life times.'"

Jane: "So?"

Mama: "So what?"

Jane: "What happened to Atlantis?"

Mama: "Right. So it turns out that Le'ah'e did not need He'ad'ra's divine will to produce a positive result and save Atlantis from sinking beneath the waves and vanishing from history.

"After hearing what the spirit said, Le'ah'e went and convinced another woman named Sa to work with her on Radea in his dreams. Sa was a member of the high council of Atlantis. And, as Le'ah'e could manifest the goddess of the earth, Sa was able to channel one of the 49 Judges of Saturn who oversee the karma and fate of all beings in the solar system.

"Le'ah'e and Sa were already highly skilled in lucid dreaming so it was easy for them to appear in Radea's dreams. And they did exactly what the spirit suggested. In his dreams, they took him into the future so that he lived many different possible endings for Atlantis.

217

"Actually, they did not have an easy time because this mean old arch demon kept trying his best to interfere with their work. But one vision of the future caught Radea's attention. He saw that if he played his cards right he would be able to establish a colony of Atlantis on another continent where it would be free of the dark order's influence.

"And having become a student of He'ad'ra and learning the cosmic language, Radea could extend his life span for hundreds of years. After the first hundred years, the scientists in that colony would advance their technologies involving transference of consciousness such that they would be able to teleport themselves back and forth between the planets circling other stars.

"The human race would then become an interstellar civilization. You see, the only reason Radea was captivated by the dark order was because of the forbidden knowledge it offered. But the language of the Creator that He'ad'ra possessed was infinitely more powerful."

Jane: "Mama."

Mama: "Yes?"

Jane: "I am going to go to sleep now. Good night."

Mama: "Good night Jane. Sweet dreams."

Now it came to pass that Zengu, a troll who lived under a bridge, had a case of acute dementia. Oh his long term memory was in good working order. He could remember exact details of experiences he had long ago. It was current events like what happened yesterday or what he had for breakfast that he could not recall.

So Zengu sent a message by carrier pigeon to the troll king. The message read, "I request I be relieved of my command. I no longer have confidence in my ability to execute your orders faithfully. I am making too many mistakes performing my duties."

The carrier pigeon returned in the late afternoon. The message read, "From the Troll King: Zengu, stand fast. Hold that bridge. You see, I am a little shorted handed at the moment as three of my best trolls recently were turned to stone when the suns' rays caught them above ground. Keep those tolls coming!"

Now it just so happened that a billy goat came by. And when Zengu demanded payment to cross the bridge the goat said with a sigh, "I already paid you. You know I cannot lie. Look into my eyes."

Zengu could see obviously that the billy goat had paid. He just could not remember when that transaction took place. So he let the goat cross over the bridge.

Later after the sun had set a vampire arrived. Zengu said, "What? Are you going to tell me you already paid?"

The vampire replied, "You know full well my clan recently negotiated a discount rate that we pay directly to the troll king on a monthly basis."

So Zengu let the vampire cross over the bridge.

Just after that a wood elf and a flower fairy stepped onto the bridge going the other way. Zengu did not bother with those kind of fairies because they are exempt from troll king decrees. You cannot tax those whose movements are neither bound by water in streams nor require a ferryman to pass over a river.

Oddly enough, later that night an incarnated mermaid came face to face with Zengu half way across the bridge. She said to him, "You poor thing. I can feel what you feel and you are not fully alive. You are half dead inside."

Zengu says, "Be that as it may, to cross this bridge you must pay."

She says, "Everything will be okay. I will have someone come by who can renegotiate your race's fate."

She then walked by the troll who did not know what to say. She was one of those incarnated mermaids who not only feel what other's feel. If she feels something is okay for her she has a way of getting others to feel the same. Namely, there are no barriers or boundaries that separate those who love; no taxes, no tolls, no need to pay, for the race of mermaids is not governed by the principle of scarcity.

Toward midnight, Zengu was checking his troll collection box and noticed something was off, for the box was quite empty. He thought to himself, "This will not do. The troll kingdom needs tolls otherwise expenses will outpace revenues."

When dawn came a human magician spoke softly to Zengu who was dozing off beneath the bridge. "Zengu," he said. "Take this coin recently minted from gold that was transformed from lead in an alchemist's lab. On its face is a sigil whose power is to manifest your deepest dreams. Treasures everywhere abound. Look around. They are easily found."

Zengu asked the mage, whose name is Smanrick, "Why are you doing this for me?"

Smanrick replied, "I call many realms my home and many races of beings consider me one of their own. It is my very nature, spontaneously and without effort, to seek to fulfill the deepest dreams in every living being. I can see what you have always wanted inside—to be as solid as the earth, undisturbed, and yet free as the sky. Negotiating tolls, taxes, and fees is your way of dealing with life's uncertainties. To be alive is to give and take, but to be fair the taking must not outweigh the giving.

"I know a human king who needs a troll like you to guard his gold hidden in a silent place beneath his castle. He also needs an accountant to keep track of his accounts.

"Don't worry. The troll king has already discussed with the human king job training for trolls such as you. If everything works out, trolls will no longer need to be homeless and destitute like those who live beneath bridges. Every castle and kingdom will have a troll who insures that their accounts are kept in balance."

"What about my dementia?" asks the troll.

"I have already taken care of that," replies the magician. "The sigil on the gold coin offers fringe benefits. There is a little-known rule of life that applies—you are as young as you feel inside."

A KNIGHT AND A DRAGON

As fairy tales go some are sad and some are happy. Some are horrific and some are wondrous. This one is of a maiden who turned herself into a dragon. Well, she had no wings or tail, no claws and no eyes that could paralyze. But she practiced "breath of fire." This was not a flame that burns but a voice and a look that can incinerate and vaporize another person's hope or happiness.

Now there was a king in that land. And his wise men pointed out to the king that something in the kingdom was wrong. There were signs and omens and a certain alignment of planets and constellations that were enough to cause a fright. The king was quick to agree, for the king could feel it in his bones or hear it as a quiet voice whispering in the halls at night.

And since the king was a man of action, he dispatched a knight. The knight was of noble birth and possessed extraordinary abilities. His task, as always, was to make things right.

Shortly after arriving on the scene, the knight looks into the woman's eyes and is mystified. Nonetheless, the knight stays focused on his mission. He recalls ancient texts and realizes what she has done to herself.

Because of her hurt and her pain, she had taken her soul out of her body and placed it inside of a black stone. And this stone has a name—it is called the stone of death, for it does not give but rather steals life from whoever comes near it.

Given the situation, the knight knew a fight would be worthless. Long established lore stated you cannot defeat a dragon such as this by sword, by spear, or by any word of power a dragon might fear.

No. The knight knew he had to exercise due diligence. He would have to avoid making assumptions and take nothing for granted. He had to justify his perception that there was a connection between this woman and a dragon.

Now at that time knights were required both to act with discretion and to use their imagination. And this knight could see with perfect clarity that before him was a human woman who somehow mysteriously was also a being of power that is an ancient, archetypal, and authentic dragon.

You may think my story is dark, dreary, and gloomy like a fable of the Brothers Grimm. But I am not making this up. I can see this dragon right here in front of me and the stone of death she has hidden somewhere most likely quite obscure.

Now the knight had a magical compass that could locate lost items or whatever he wanted. Using it, he followed the direction it indicated until he came to a cave where the black stone was hidden. To keep it short, he found the stone deep in the cave. It was sitting on a pedestal made out of an ancient, petrified tree.

As the knight drew near, the black stone spoke in a deep, challenging voice, "Tell me the taste of the elixir of eternal beauty that Persephone gave to Psyche and which Psyche drank at the risk of her life. Answer my riddle if you wish to complete your quest. I am only asking for the meaning of life and of death."

And when the stone was done speaking all manner of beings came out of the stone and filled up the room so that the knight had hardly left any elbow room. There was a gorgon rather testy, a harpy with very bad breath, a banshee with a most grating voice, a griffin who was itchy, vampires who were thirsty, and werewolves who were nasty, a miniature kraken out of its depth though still quite slimy, and a few medusas to boot who had plenty of reasons to be unhappy. And they all spoke in unison with the same words, "We too enjoin you to answer the question the stone has set before you."

And the knight replies and these are his words which issued from his lips. They were spoken with the same conviction that Winston Churchill used to command his nation in its darkest hour so that the people might be inspired.

The knight said, "It matters not in what realm you dwell or in what form you travel as long as you are free in your soul. Then depression and despair cannot find you; death cannot bind you; and the restrictions and limitations of life cannot confuse you.

"In spite of what theologians may say, no one guards heaven's gates. No one blocks the way. Heaven shall come down to earth. There are no locks and no keys. Everyone is free to enter.

"The heart is an open space that accepts all things. But in the depths of the heart there is an ecstasy of such beauty and grace those who know this taste death cannot embrace.

"I tell you love commands every being to awake, to attain absolute freedom, and in the end to perceive that you and I and every other are one without separation."

At this point the harpy breaks the silence and asks, "Perhaps there are a few things you left out?"

And the knight says, "Go on? Like what?"

The harpy replies, "To fill the earth with justice is also a noble quest."

And the knight responds, "You are right. And in pursuit of that I will do my best."

And with the same tone of voice the kraken asks, "What about an innocence and love so pure that malice dissolves in their presence as if it was never there?"

The knight says, "Yes. Yes. You and I are on the same page with this."

And one of the medusas say, "Those who look into my eyes die of stone cold fright."

And the knight replies, "That is the test you have set and I agree with you on this: to learn to be free of fear—we all need to get there."

And the gorgon chimes in, "Horror and terror are a part of life as breath and heartbeat strive to unite."

And the knight says, "Horror and terror as well as beauty and love—to accept the best and also the worst in life is required for those who would be guided from above."

The banshee blurts out with a wail and a cry, "To die is to leave your life behind."

The knight replies, "And for every ending there is a new beginning."

The griffin, with wings and the beak of a bird and tail and claws of a lion, says, "The heart that soars high no doubt shall be torn and ravaged by betrayal and lies."

And the knight says, "'The broken heart shall mend but never much too soon;' to heal others is to heal one's own wounds."

The vampire says, "In my eyes, the living are already half dead and their lives will soon come to an end."

The knight says, "Every true warrior knows that to be fully alive you have to be ready to die."

And the werewolf says, "In my clan in Ireland, the gift is passed down through the blood."

And the knight says, "Yes, father to son and mother to daughter—the spirit in one gives birth to the spirit in the other."

And upon speaking these words the monsters disappear one by one until they were all gone. And then the stone turns to dust and rises up as black smoke, fading away and is no more.

Soon after the dragon woman awakens with her soul intact and back inside of her. She shines bright and new as dawn and has the softness and sweet scent of a flower. And so it was that the dragon woman, now a maiden again, became known throughout the entire kingdom as being so vivacious and serene that she could charm the soul of any man. And anyone suffering from despair, sorrow, loss, or pain she could free or heal them, for she set before their feet a path of beauty and wonder that was both enchanting and captivating.

The knight returns to the king who suitably rewards him and then asks that he fulfill other missions. The services of this knight are always in demand, for this is the nature of human existence—there shall always be new quests as long as the human heart remains restless.

PART VII

CELESTIAL BUREAUCRACY

A kasha refers to the fifth element alongside earth, air, fire, and water. Akasha also refers to a plane or level of consciousness, as in the physical, etheric, astral, mental, and spiritual or akashic planes. In both examples, it is formless and timeless; it is a state of awareness penetrating through space and time without restriction.

A man walks down a corridor and pauses in front of the secretary's desk.

Secretary: (Looking up). "Yes? Can I help you?"

Man: "I want to set up my own fairy kingdom."

Secretary: "Oh, wouldn't that be wonderful! Let me see. Just a moment."

She reaches into a drawer in the desk and takes out a piece of paper as she says, "Here it is."

She checks a few squares next to questions and then hands the form to the man as she says, "Take this form and go to room 1A and speak with Rev. Bilgray. He will answer all your questions."

The man knocks on the door of 1A.

Rev. Bilgray: "Come in."

The man enters and sits in a chair in front of Bilgray's desk

Rev. Bilgray: "Now then, how may I help you?

The man hands Bilgray the form.

Rev. Bilgray: "It says here you wish to construct your own astral realm, a fairy kingdom, to be exact. Oh. Won't that be wonderful!"

Man: "Yes. I am very excited about this project."

Rev. Bilgray, after gazing carefully at the man, says: "You seem to possess all the qualifications and meet all the requirements. I just have a few minor questions before you receive your official certification."

Man: "Please. I am happy to answer your questions."

Rev. Bilgary: "Have you had any demonic contact in your last four incarnations?"

Man: "No. Nothing I can recall.

Rev. Bilgray: "Are you currently subject any kind of karmic restrictions or do you have any pacts with any spirits positive or negative?"

Man: "No and no."

"Rev. Bilgray: "And next we want to know what resources you have at your disposal. To maintain your fairy kingdom will require substantial amounts of energy. Are you, for example, a trained hermetic magician having reached chapter seven of Initiation into Hermetics?"

Man: "I have never heard of Initiation into Hermetics. I don't even know what hermetics is. Do you suggest I buy the book?"

Bilgray: "No. No. Just asking. Do you get tired easily? Have trouble sleeping at night? And do you lucid dream at least once a week?"

Man: "No. I feel as if I am still 26. I fall asleep with great ease and sleep until early morning. And yes I often have lucid dreams. I can lucid dream at will in fact. And not only that. I can meet other people or spirits in my dreams if I make an effort."

Rev. Bilgray: "Very good. Now then, can you through concentration change the temperature of a room you are in up or down by three to five degrees?"

Man: "I never thought of trying that. Should I?"

Rev. Bilgray: "Just asking. And do you have a congregation, sangha, ashram, temple, or do you practice ritual magic in any kind of group?"

Man: "Well. I used to practice the Golden Dawn rituals. I did a little reiki. I hang out with a yoga group that practices pranayama. I used to attend all the local Tibetan Buddhist pujas.

"I did Tai Chi Chuan for thirty years. A little Pilates."

Rev. Bilgray. "Yes. Yes. That is all very nice. But what I am getting at is do you know how to create enough energy to set up and to sustain an astral realm? You see, we get complaints about fairy kings and queens establishing astral kingdoms. Some of them run short on their energy supplies. Then they start raiding other kingdoms or else they vampirize humans in the physical world when people are asleep and dreaming."

Man: "Oh no! I would never do anything unethical. I assure you my intentions are pure from the word go. I am not like humans who take more than they give.

"And I will neither kidnap nor trick anyone into entering my kingdom to do my bidding or simply to have someone to lord over who isn't a figment of my own imagination."

Rev. Bilgray: "You look like an honest man. If I might ask? What gave you the idea of creating your own fairy realm?"

Man: "To be honest? I got tired of watching Netflix, HBO, Showtime, movie 25, and amazon prime."

Rev. Bilgray: "Have you thought of writing a novel to share your dreams, inspiration, and imagination with others?"

Man: "I am planning to do just that. But I want to offer my readers something more than a brief entertaining experience. I want those who are open to suggestion to be able to go to sleep at night and, through dreams or even day dreams, visit an entire world that is autonomous and that offers vast horizons to explore."

Rev. Bilgray: "But this is primarily for you, right? Like what do you yourself want?"

Man: "I want to live and breathe in a world of my own creation where the air is saturated with inspiration, where love is like a sea that surrounds and flows through every being.

"I want to look down inside my body and see light shining as dazzling as the sun. I want to feel joined with my opposite, the feminine essence and the perfection of love.

"I want to heal with a thought or transform others with a glance or a single spoken word. I want the beauty of the earth and the sky and all the stars at night to shine back at me when I look into another person's eyes.

"I want to feel one with every being in my kingdom, animal, human, and divine. I want to work together in harmony with others to make the world new each day. I want to be surrounded by colors that are a thousand times more beautiful than what I see on earth.

"I want to welcome others into my kingdom that wish to experience an absolute contentment from within that is one with the universe. And I want others to experience what I experience with ease—that when we as a group meditate together in my kingdom we feel one with every other being that loves throughout the entire universe."

Rev. Bilgray: "That is all very generous and inspirational. You intend then to invite others into your fairy kingdom? I mean, most people who apply for a fairy kingdom license usually set up the entire kingdom around their own imagination. It does not occur to them to have other living souls present. Consequently, the population of that kingdom is then a figment of their own imagination. In this way they can maintain absolute sovereignty. Until of course they get bored of the bardo state and decide to reincarnate.

"Let me just ask you outright. Are you one of those who are behind the scenes planning to upgrade your fairy kingdom into some sort of religious heaven? You know, we get a lot of complaints from the fundamentalists in all religions about cult heavens.

"People die. They check in. And then they discover they can never leave. The "heaven" requires fresh energy to function. Otherwise the light starts losing its color. The smells grow stale. Sounds of birds and music begin to be drowned out by white noise.

"It is just not good for the astral plane to have these toxic waste dumps of unfiltered emotions present that might end up contaminating the other heavens and kingdoms. You understand what I am saying?"

Man: "Let me be perfectly clear. I am not interested in setting up a religious heaven. That is exactly what I want to get away from. I want to invite my friends and those who love to simply share soul to soul and heart to heart in a nurturing and harmonious manner."

Rev. Bilgray: "Very well then. Here is your license for your fairy kingdom.

"I have to disclose at this point that we here in the Akashic Department of Fairy Kingdoms actually have no legal authority to regulate or to accept or reject any applications. Whatever karmic issues come up in how you run your kingdom are overseen directly by the 49 Judges of Saturn.

"All the same, the Judges like us to clarify people's intentions and remind them to always maintain a surplus of energy and ascribe to high ethics. This is important because lately some of the religious heavens have been unable to keep up with maintenance and repairs."

Rev. Bilgray stands up and shakes the man's hand and then says, "And if you don't mind I think I would like to drop in and see how well you are able to perfect your vision of uniting with all beings who love throughout the universe. I have heard of that. Just haven't yet experienced it firsthand."

Man: "Of course. I would love to see you again. Perhaps I could utilize you as a consultant from time to time? You must have quite a few tips to offer from all your observations of what is going on in the astral plane of the earth?"

Rev. Bilgray: "It would be my pleasure. And best of luck to you."

Man: "Thank you."

Man: "Excuse me."Divine Being: "You are hereby excused."

Man: "Is this the Akashic Department of Customer Service?"

Divine Being: "That is exactly what it is."

Man: "And can I submit complaints here?"

Divine Being: "We don't call them complaints. We call them opportunities for improvement."

Man: "I ...." (divine being interrupting).

Divine Being: "If you could keep it short, concise, and to the point. It really helps. Even though we run on non-linear time, time is still priceless."

Man: "Right. To the point. I have noticed that Homo sapiens is haunted by an ancient loneliness. There is a sense of being abandoned because when we put on a human body at birth we must take it off again when we die. That loneliness of the soul—that death is inevitable—no love can cure. No matter how many friends we have or how deep our love with another, no one can stand by our side as we transition from this world to the next."

Divine Being: "As a matter of fact, without a physical body you are not in this world but a spirit on the astral plane.

"Have you been reading The Operations Manual for Human Beings? You are very articulate. The abandonment and loneliness you mention are indeed characteristics of human existence.

"Now then, do you have a suggestion to improve things or are you here today just to hear yourself talking?"

Man: "I would like a way to solve this problem of abandonment and loneliness that is inherent in human existence."

Divine Being: "Ah. I love short, to the point, and concise statements. Very well."

The divine being waves his hand in the air.

"There. What do you see?"

Man: "You have turned me into Dante. I see all worlds appearing before my eyes: time past, present, and the future of the physical world. Linear and non-linear time.

"I see those who are now alive. And I see all realms of the dead, those going into the light and those who linger as hungry or haunting ghosts. There are those waiting to be born and there are places where the lineage masters roam. There are the realms of the elemental beings who possess immortality. There are the bardo states, heavens and hells men through their imaginations create.

"I see dreamtimes of different races from the Aborigines, the Sioux, the Japanese, the English—all racial and ethnic places where people go to feel at home when they are dead. I see many mansions of the soul. I see races unborn that will one day appear on earth. I see all manner of beings—unicorns, dragons, hobgoblins, wood elves, kingdoms of fairy, magical kingdoms created by magicians and divine beings.

"There is a time to be born and a time to die. How is this a solution to my existential problem? I thought you might just take away my hypersensitivity so I can be blind and happy like other humans."

Divine Being: "It is quite possible that if you had a lover whose touch says in effect, 'I feel what you feel. I will be at your side and with you wherever you may go regardless of not knowing in what way you are transforming.'

"That touch by another dissolves the ancient loneliness that haunts the human soul and through it all sense of abandonment vanishes forever."

Man: "I don't get it. Are you offering me such a lover who will love me in this life and in every other?"

Divine Being: "No. In your case, such a simple remedy would not suffice. Let me ask you this: Why have I opened your eyes so you can see clearly all realms of the soul where all beings dwell or pass through?"

Man: "Ah. Yes. Why didn't I think of this? I am to be this person for any other who is in need of someone to walk by his or her side so that loneliness ceases to exist on this planet forever."

Divine Being: "Exactly. And if I might say, I like the way your mind works. Drop by anytime."

A man knocks on a door. An angelic voice inside says, "Come in." The man enters and the angel indicates with his hand that he take a seat.

Angel: "How may I help you?"

Man: "Is this the Akashic Department of Guardian Angels?"

Angel: "Why yes it is."

Man: "And can you certify, authorize, or otherwise commission the creation of guardian angels, for example, by upgrading a human being so he can act as a divine spirit with a sacred mission to watch over and guide incarnated souls on earth?"

Angel: "Of course. You have come to the right place. The concept of guardian angels originated with me. I was the first one to propose that an angel be assigned to each human being on earth. Life on this planet can get pretty messy without a little help, don't you think?

"But why don't we stop beating around the bush. Tell me exactly what you want."

Man: "I would like to apply to become a guardian angel."

Angel: "Are you sure you are in the right department? Because down the hall and the first door on the left is the Akashic Department of Spirit Guides. I think you would find their work a whole lot more satisfying and, when it comes down to it, a much better fit if I might say so."

Man: "No. No. I appreciate spirit guides and all that they do. I really do. But that is definitely not what I want. Not my style at all."

Angel: "And what exactly is your style?"

Man: "I want the guardian angel capacity to whisper in someone's ear as a still, quiet voice—the voice of a person's own conscience seeking to reduce that individual's suffering on earth. I want to get through to people using promptings, intuition, dreams, and hint at, even suggest, the best way to fulfill their path of life. I want the power to bless individual's lives in every aspect.

"I want to remind individuals of the infinite possibilities that surround them and that there are no limitations set on what they may accomplish while they are here on earth. And I want the full authority to intervene when they are in danger. And at times, if they are mortally injured, I want to exercise the option of converting an otherwise certain death into a near death experience so they return to life with a new purpose."

Angel: "You definitely have been reading The Guardian Angel's Handbook.

"Now then, what makes you think you are qualified for this upgrade?"

Man: "I have studied the five elements in nature so they are now a part of my soul."

Angel: "Why don't you tell me about that?"

Man: "I met a girl. She was a sylph incarnated in human form. I did not know about air spirits at the time. I suffered horribly for the next twenty years longing to find in myself what she had briefly awoken in me."

Angel: "And what did she awake in you so briefly and painfully?"

Man: "She gave me a taste and longing to make absolute freedom a part of myself. Because I did not have the faintest clue as to how to embody the essence of sylphs, I kept making the same mistakes over and over. My life was Groundhog Day until I came to sense the air in the sky flows through my chest. Its winds are my breath.

"Now hurricanes count me as an old friend. I speak their language as we communicate mind to mind. And I have the air element's artistic bent of being completely detached and in the same moment hyper sensitive to every sensory impression. Now stories flow through my soul like water flowing through a stream. Like Shakespeare, I sense in each person I meet an original story, a drama that opens when they walk onto the stage of life and unfolds through desire and dream and amid limitations they struggle to be free."

Angel: "Yes. Yes. Go on. I am all ears."

Man: "I met another girl. She was a mermaid but I did not know that at the time. Just touching her skin I felt I had become the sea. Dreams of peace, happiness, tenderness, contentment, and satisfaction flowed through me.

"But when I was not around her I suffered terribly. I experienced physical withdrawal symptoms and was disoriented. The timeless realm that she had come from kept calling to me, inviting me, to put aside my human identity and to become pure love. This enchantment was two sided. One side was bliss and the other side was feeling half dead as if I had lost my chance to be fully alive.

"This conflict persisted until I found inside myself the bubbling, splashing, laughing explosions of joy in a waterfall, the surging, swirling, soothing, and nurturing life in a stream, the cleansing of snow melting in spring, the Arctic Bay with its dreams of wild purity, the raging waves of the North Atlantic hungry to find another to unite with, and the sea with its dream of being one with the all the stars in the sky.

"Now a sea of love flows through my soul and extends outward surrounding the entire planet. I find the purest and best dreams in another's soul and seek with all my being to assist in fulfilling them."

Angel: "You are definitely on a roll. Don't stop now."

Man: "I met a girl. She was a gnome, the earth itself in human form. I did not know it at the time. Sitting beside her I felt the silence of a cave deep beneath a mountain chain. For her to be alive is to work at what you love and to do it with all of your heart. She had that sense of well-being that feels that everything good in life will come to you without effort in its own time.

"But I suffered terribly when she was no longer at my side. And then I found her silence inside of me. In the dead of night and in a deep hidden stillness, a vibration of the ground entered my feet and passed upward through my body.

"And then I heard the song of the earth. The beauty was staggering. Now the enduring silence of the earth is in my feelings and my thoughts—the fields with their abundant harvests, the solidity of mountains and granite cliffs, the Vishnu schist, the rock solid peace. The girl and the earth itself are within and are a part of me."

Angel: "Not bad. Not bad at all for a human. Go on."

Man: "I met another girl. I did not know it but she was a salamander, a fire spirit, who had taken on human form. She was the incarnation of a super volcano.

"Like a complete fool I was attracted to her primordial hunger to expand and to acquire power. Her blind, primal drive was to take control of everything that limits you, to test all boundaries, and to assail every obstacle until every problem in life is solved and the unknown has been taken hold of and converted into a home."

Angel: "Biting off more than you can chew, were you?"

Man: "That is an understatement."

Angel: "I am sitting on the edge of my chair. What happened?"

Man: "I was devastated. Such women are warriors. But affection and love are not their game. How do you take fire into your arms and speak words of such power you turn fire into a friend and a lover?"

Angel: "Didn't work out then?"

Man: "The opposite was the case. Justice requires the union of love and power. I found in fire the source of all light. That source is now within me and with it from darkness I create light and from malice I can create chivalry and true nobility. I can enter the heart of any man and speak with his own voice hidden in the core of his being. To fill the earth with justice is my dream."

Angel: "Might I ask—In your mind, is your desire to become a guardian angel a natural consequence of your study of the four elements or is this an idea that was in the back of your mind for a large part of your life?"

Man: "It was when the worst in life kept visiting me that I realized something was wrong. Suffering terribly is not the best thing to combine with love. So I realized I had to take responsibility for my actions. I had to step back, to understand patterns of behavior, circumstances, and timing. And I had to learn to be perfectly clear about the outcomes I wanted to manifest."

Angel: "Well, to be honest with you, with over seven billion souls incarnated on earth we are running a little short of guardian angels.

"Now follow my thinking on this. Would it not be in your best interest, my best interest, and the best interest of the human race as well for you to be a little more than a guardian angel?

"You see, what we really need is someone incarnated like you to open a magic university to train others to do what you yourself have learned to do. In this way, more needs are met. Suffering on earth is reduced to a greater extent. And the divine world and human world can work together more efficiently and with greater satisfaction."

Man: "That sounds great. I will need funding of course and a core team of highly skilled magicians to work with on this project."

Angel: "Sure. Whatever you want. Just ask. And good luck to you."

A man knocks on the door. Divine Being: "Don't just stand out there. Come in."

The man enters the room and sits down.

Man: "Is this the Akashic Dating Service?"

Divine Being: "Why yes it is. How can I help you?"

Man: "I would like a perfect soul mate. No, actually a twin flame. Well, maybe more. How about a divine partner with whom I can celebrate all mysteries?"

Divine Being: "We are not called the Akashic Dating Service for nothing. I offer all forms of love from the lowest animalistic, libidinous, and enthralling erotic to the highest union with divinity —ineffable and beyond human understanding, though still very real. It is all right here ready to go. You only need ask."

Man: "Great. Because I have had such a struggle you know." Divine Being: "If you want to reflect on or revisit your struggles in the past, that would be the Department of Akashic Records. First door down the hall and on the left. They are really quite good you know—they can reproduce the exact eidetic memory in full color and wrap around sound including every sensory sensation, perception, thought, and feeling that you have ever experienced in the past."

Man: "No, no. I want a perfect partner for celebrating the mysteries of life. I am not here to talk about the past." Divine Being: "Good. Because in this room there is only now. Past and future do not exist. Okay then, let's proceed. Give me more details about what you want.

"Like are you after the kind of rapport with another that is so perfect that you feel one with each other? How about an ecstasy in which there is no separation between the two of you? Or maybe just that physical sensation of closeness in which you feel you live and breathe each other's presence in every moment?"

Man: "Oh, those sound very romantic."

Divine Being: "You know, everything I just described is a Gemini approach to relationships. You might prefer the Taurus approach. For example, Taurus offers a feeling of being one with each other and one with the universe in the same moment. There is a very solid bond drawing you to each other like the pull of gravity."

Man: "I hadn't thought about that."

Divine Being: "Then again, I could refer you to a Capricorn relationship that orbits around power. How about a nice relationship in which the woman and you feel there is nothing else that exists when you are with each other. And to boot she furthers you work in life increasing your productivity tenfold. That is very Capricorn—being productive, meeting goals, and accomplishing your mission. We here in the Departments of Akasha really appreciate people who get their missions done on time."

Man: "Now I am confused."

Divine Being: "On second thought, perhaps something more along the lines of Scorpio. Some say Scorpio invented sex and for that reason Scorpio has its own Akashic Department. Just a little farther down the hall and to the right is the Scorpio counselor. There you will experience the bliss of kundalini rising through your chakras until in your crown chakra you and your consort are united in divine rapture just like Shiva and Shakti. As rapture goes it is hard to beat a feeling of being brighter than ten thousand suns."

Man: "Now you are making fun of me."

Divine Being: "Not at all. We just have so much to offer up here in akasha. And, to tell you the truth, we are sometimes bored to tears because so few human beings ever bother to investigate their options when it comes to pleasure, love, and romance."

Man: "Perhaps if you actually showed me my ideal kind of woman I might have a better sense of how to proceed."

Divine Being: "Perhaps. Gaze into this crystal ball. What you see within it are the nations of earth and those dots of various colored light are the partners that are right for you. Now the brighter lights are more right but, trust me, you will be happy with any of them."

Man: "What about that one right there?" The man points his finer at an opal light on the West coast of the U.S.

Divine Being: "Excellent choice. Now that young lady is very special and I haven't mentioned that kind of love yet. With her your love is like a sea without shores. You feel so much a part of each other and so innocent too that there is no longer a you. Just a feeling of love flowing without end. Of course, it goes without saying that this love includes a profound state of rapture and a wonderful feeling of release.

Though we like people who complete their missions in life, this love is under the sign of Cancer. And Cancer has that special gift of knowing through pure feeling when something is right. For the constellation of Cancer, those who possess deep happiness accomplish so much more in life than they would by embodying any other virtue."

Man: "Oh, she seems perfect. That is the girl I want."

Divine Being: "Well, sir, it is easy enough for me to introduce you to this woman. But you see this is the 'Akashic Dating Service.' You do not get something for nothing. You have to become the love you seek.

"Oh I could set you up with her. But after a time the love would inevitably falter, grow dim, and fail. And that is because love of this caliber is not something that just happens. You have to create it, otherwise you would not be getting your money's worth, would you?

"Experience gives you a taste. But the taste is only a first step. You still have to become a master chef, not just someone who orders a dish off a menu even if it is a five star restaurant."

Man: "I get it now. You have a class of instruction I am supposed to take.

Divine Being: "Exactly. We are teachers assigned by Divine Providence to assist anyone on earth who drops in. In fact, each day every one of these kinds of love I have described and many others emanate through the entire planet earth for anyone who is sensitive, imaginative, or receptive enough to sense them. We like to say, 'If you can imagine it so it feels real, then you can make it real.'"

Man: "Okay then. You introduce me to the girl and I will train in any way you require that divine love might manifest on earth."

Divine Being: "Go through the door to your left. She is waiting for you in the next room."

Man: "Excuse me."Being: "Yes? Can I help you?" Man: "I hope so. You are the first real thing I have run into here."

Being: "Go on."

Man: "Look. I have this overwhelming feeling I am supposed to go into the light. I mean, there is this dazzling bright circle of white light I see occasionally hovering in front of me. And I feel certain I am supposed to enter it.

"But every time I try to move toward it, it disappears."

Being: "Ah. Here is the deal. You have to let go of the life you have left behind. I mean, you realize you are dead, right?"

Man: "Yes. I understand that. I am dead and there is no going back."

"And I have figured out I am caught here in this dreamlike place of fantastic visions where everything I imagine appears around me with perfect clarity. But all the same I understand that everything I see is an illusion, a product of my subconscious desires and unmet longings.

"So I get it. It is time to move on. Wait. What is this about letting go of the life I left behind? I thought I had already done that."

Being: "You have to let go of your desires, everything you wanted, everything you were invested in and that gave your life meaning. You have to forget about all your triumphs and failures. Those women you slept with. Those women you wanted but who never responded. You know, all those things that were so real to you and which you did everything in your power to hold onto.

"Let go of it all. It is gone. It is over. Done. No more. Let go."

Man: "Look. I am on the same page as you. But here is the problem. If I put off to the side all my desires, my hopes and dreams, my relationships with others, and the things I fought so hard to achieve, there would be nothing left of me. Nothing.

"What then is left of me to enter the light?"

Being: "Well, there is giving and receiving. Caring. Sharing heart to heart and soul to soul. Even though you are now dead, these things keep you alive."

Man: "What you are saying is that this going into the light is about the heart then and not so much about the mind?"

Being: "Let me put it this way: when you are in touch with your deepest feelings all your dreams will manifest spontaneously. What you are then is a natural part of the unfolding of the universe."

Man: "Ah. Look at that! The light!"

The man enters the light and is gone.

Being: (sighing) "Humans!"

A Few Brief Questions Before Going into the Light

Administrator: "Excuse me Sir." Man: "Yes." Administrator: "I would like to congratulate you. You are all cleared to go into the Light. But if you do not mind, I have a few brief questions I would like to ask you."

Man: "Is there a problem? I mean, when the light appears in front of me the whole point is that I enter it and that is that. It is a personal thing, something spontaneous and natural."

"After all, it took some work to get to here. I had to let go of all my attachments, social connections, affiliations, accomplishments, and self-image—the many roles I have played. I am dead and finally I accept that and I am now ready to move on."

Administrator: "You are quite right of course. And I do not want to subtract in any way from the purity of what you are about to experience. It is just that, due to complaints and suggestions for improvements, we have upgraded the 'going into the light' experience.

"Perhaps you would like to be informed of some of the options we now offer for those who are in your position. I assure you that in no way will you experience less than what you would have received with the older version of going into the light."

Man: "Go ahead. I am willing to listen."

Administrator: "There are just four points on my check list. The first point pertains to power, purpose, and destiny.

"In your next incarnation, would you consider taking a role of great responsibility? Perhaps you would like to be in a position to change the world in dramatic ways? To do this I can place you in a family and circumstances where you will rise to the highest levels of power in your society. From that position, you will be able to eliminate corruption in your nation's government and establish justice throughout the world.

"On the other hand, perhaps you are more interested in the default setting for power, purpose, and destiny. You might want to just be a deacon in a church, a community organizer, a member of a neighborhood board, or the president of the local PTA. You have any preferences along these lines?"

Man: "I was thinking of maybe being a life guard. I always wanted to work near the water. And I love the beach. Throw in a lot of surfing too if that is okay."

Administrator: "Sure thing. I will mark that down here —'beach bum.'

"Now the second item on my list pertains to wisdom. You see there is a stillness that embraces the universe. From out of it arises all harmony and wisdom through which every conflict is resolved and every problem is solved.

"Along these lines, you might like to be born with special siddhis involving telepathy. We have a special offer that is appropriate in your case in which you are able to imitate the brain waves in other people's minds. In this way you will not only be able to read their minds and think their thoughts. You will understand the ways in which their thoughts arise.

"And, in addition, you will be able to link different individuals' minds together so they form one group consciousness in which each individual's experiences are fully understood by the others in the group. This is an invaluable skill for solving problems in communication and expressing yourself under all social conditions and circumstances.

"On the other hand, you might prefer the default setting for mental activity in which over decades you arrive at where you can understand both sides of any argument. And with sufficient experience you may even develop a judicial temperament in which you acquire a tolerance for ambiguity and formulate your judgments based on evidence, intentions, and circumstances."

Man: "I am wondering if you have any options where I can think without using thoughts? You know, sitting on the beach in that life guard tower or out there surfing, I want to take in the whole experience without being dragged down by the clichés and thoughts of the superego that so many people adopt as the absolute truth."

Administrator: "Very good. I will put down here on my form —'Requests ability to perceive, evaluate, and act without the need to use thoughts or ideas.'

"Now the third item on my list involves love. We can in fact now offer to each person the opportunity to experience the one, all-embracing love that unites all other forms and aspects of love within it. This love reigns over the entire universe. It governs and oversees the unfolding of all destinies of all individuals, beings, and galactic civilizations.

"Irresistible in attraction, all desires arise from it and are fulfilled through it. It is a perfect empathy in which you are able to feel what any other being feels and to experience any other person's life as if their memories are your own experiences.

"On the other hand, the default setting for love involves the same oh same oh grow up missing key elements in your development, hit puberty, discover the opposite gender, have your hormones and anatomy determine 90% of your feelings and actions, have relationships most of which are unsatisfactory, get married, have kids, experience terrible frustration and loneliness amid all of this, and in the end learn that you are responsible for your own happiness.

"Have any preferences?"

Man: "You know, the primary fringe benefit of being in a physical body is you get to have sex. Can you mark down there that as a world level surfer I get to have sex with unbelievably attractive, nubile, and sexy women who get turned on just by being around me?"

Administrator: "You got it. And now for the fourth item. This pertains to your accomplishments in life. One aspect of the physical world and of being incarnated is that you are able to improve the world through your work in a way that enriches the lives of all who follow after you.

"There are of course no limitations place on what you may accomplish in life. Some people find work that they love doing and they do it with all of their heart. Time does not matter to them, for they experience a quiet ecstasy in their pursuits.

"You can for example discover new things, make new inventions, innovate in creative ways, or bring new art into the world like Shakespeare, Van Gogh, or Beethoven.

"You can also be blessed by luck and good fortune, be anointed so to speak so that the deepest purposes of life come alive in you.

"On the other hand, the default setting is that alpha males and females, institutions and corporations determine the jobs you take, what you are paid, and the kind of output that derives from your work."

Man: "Stories."

Administrator: "What about stories?"

Man: "Stories are the oldest form of culture, right?"

Administrator: "That is correct. Where are you going with this?"

Man: "I want to tell stories around camp fires at beach parties and luaus. I want to tell stories with such art and charisma that the characters in my stories come to life.

"These characters then enter the dreams of those who hear my words, introducing them to multi-dimensional reality and non-linear time. Thereafter they have lucid dreams in which they perceive there is no separation between the lives they have lived before and the lives they will live in the future.

"In fact, I want the voice of the ancient bard which is so imbued with magic and enchantment that when I tell a story people wake up, their eyes are opened, and they see through the veils that separate the worlds of form from the realms of pure light.

"I want to convince my listeners that they do not have to wait until they are dead to go into the light and receive these upgrades you are now offering me.

"I want them to realize right now while they are still alive that by contemplation they can unite themselves to omnipotent power, all-embracing love, cosmic harmony, and the will to change the world—that these capacities are a part of being alive and are available in every moment of time."

Administrator: "Yes. I think that is doable. I will mark —'speaks with voice of the ancient bard'—down here on my check list for your next life. And may I say, it is an absolute pleasure working with you."

Man: "See you around."

The man turns and enters the light.

AFTERWORD

In writing, the artist can take a problem that has no solution and "study" it or express it so that his situation is communicated to others. Dramatized, the act of sharing in itself is a kind of healing.

I imagine worlds in which a character I create lives out my problem in a different context. And by observing how he deals with it, I can then live through his experience and learn what he has learned.

And sometimes I imagine worlds where others have solved the problems I have. It is then like an alternate reality, a parallel world. I look upon these individuals' lives and say, "Ah. Yes. That is what I might have done here with a little more time, 'with a greater will and a greater love.'"

And then it becomes okay, for I see that in future lives I will have already perfected the mission I was sent into the world to fulfill. And I realize deep inside that that future life is in a sense already real. It is alive within me right now. And then I feel whole and I am restored to harmony.

To write words forged from the bliss of imagination is to take into one's hands the powers of creation.

ABOUT THE AUTHOR

William Mistele graduated from Wheaton College in Wheaton, Illinois, with a bachelor's degree in philosophy and a minor in economics. At that time, he began studying esoteric, oral traditions. In genuine mythology, individuals come into contact with the creative powers of the universe. In esoteric traditions, words and language possess symbolic and imaginative qualities. To understand an idea is to experience it from within. This involves a lifelong, transforming journey—if you change the self, you change the world.

As part of his field research, he lived in a Tibetan Buddhist monastery in Berkeley, California. He next studied Hopi Indian culture and language at the University of Arizona, where he received a master's degree in linguistics. At that time he became the only student of a Hopi Indian shaman.

While living in Tucson, Arizona, he began studying the Western hermetic traditions and the nature religions of Wicca and Druidry. He worked with a number of extremely gifted psychics and parapsychologists whose primary focus was on experimentation and research. He also practiced evocation with a Sufi master.

He moved to Hawaii in 1982. There he studied with the relocated abbot of a Taoist monastery that existed for over two thousand years in China, with a Vietnamese Zen master, and with one of the foremost Tai Chi Chuan masters of China.

Since 1975, he has been a steadfast student of the system of initiation taught by the Czech magician Franz Bardon, who died in the fifties. Bardon's mission was to offer a system of self-initiation that leads to direct contact with the spirits of nature (mermaids, sylphs, gnomes, and salamanders) and the spirits of the planetary spheres.

The author calls himself a spiritual anthropologist. Expanding on Bardon's purposes, he has sought to integrate into his practice the wisdom of all traditions. To this end, he has created a new genre of modern fairy tales. These stories are not about belief or faith but direct experience. They open gates to other realms where we discover the keys to what is missing from life.

To find out more about William Mistele or to send comments please view the following links:

Video poems - Williammistele.com/videopoems.html
Facebook - Facebook.com/williamrmistele
Website: Williamrmistele.com
Contact: pyrhums@yahoo.com